Clothed

In Thunder

In the Shadow
of the Cedar
Book Two

Sheila Hollinghead

*This is a work of fiction. Names, characters, places, and events are the products of the author's imagination **or** are used fictitiously*

For my dear brother, Fred, who has been a great source of encouragement from day one, my sons, Ray and Lee, my daughter-in-law, Leigh, and my grandchildren.
A special thanks to Sabre whose picture graces the cover.
Thanks also to all who helped me on my journey to publication.

May they always find rest
in the shadow of the cedar.

Chapter 1--The Leaving
1937

The cool morning air did little to clear my head. Although only the middle of October, the temperature plunged last night, and I shivered in the shade of the cedar tree. Another step and the sunlight would have warmed me. Yet, the shade kept me rooted to the spot and calmed me. Still, thoughts swirled like clothes stirred in a washtub.

I did the right thing. Momma needed help. And there had been no alternative.

Living here with Aunt Liza and Uncle Howard was the only way. The dream of marrying Michael was just that--a dream. I was just fifteen. Still, like Momma had said, lots of girls married at fifteen. But I wanted more than just marriage and children.

Momma said book learning put crazy notions in my head. Maybe she was right. To be a veterinarian involved a lot of work and expense. And, even if I made it through school, no one would employ a woman vet. *At least, that's what people said.*

Maybe it would be best to forget about school and marry Michael. But what would become of *his* plans to attend college?

As if on cue, Michael came out of my uncle's shop. He spotted me and walked over to where I stood.

My heart quickened when he reached to take my hand.

"Good morning, Jay. You're up early."

His hand felt so warm and comforting that I moved closer to him. "I couldn't sleep."

His warm brown eyes studied me. "Worried?"

"A little." I reached with my free hand to break a branch from the tree. I twirled it through my fingers, releasing the cedar scent. "Am I doing the right thing?"

Part of me wanted Michael to rescue me, to sweep me away, to shelter me forever. I held my breath.

"Yes, you're doing the right thing." He pulled away from me and held me at arm's length. "I did a lot of thinking last night. You're right. We're too young to get married, and, besides, a few months isn't long. Soon I'll be back and going to college. We'll be able to see each other more then."

I sighed, slightly disappointed. What did I expect? For him to say he couldn't live without me, that he would never leave me? Yet, I knew he was just being practical, that he was saying the right thing.

I nodded and released the cedar branch that landed underfoot. He grabbed my hand, and, with our fingers entwined, we headed for the house.

Smells of cooked bacon and ham drifted to us. The table almost groaned under the mass of food.

Aunt Liza, presiding over the feast, beamed at us. Zeke was already seated at the table, and I kissed the top of my little brother's head before taking my seat.

"Howard," Aunt Liza called. "Get in here before the biscuits get cold."

Uncle Howard came into the kitchen and slipped a suspender into place. He took his seat at the head of the table and grinned at us. "This table's been empty of young'ns too long. I'm mighty glad y'all are here."

His kind words brought a smile to my face and helped beat down the fear threatening to surface.

We joined hands, and Uncle Howard blessed our meal.

The freshly churned butter melted on the biscuits and dripped onto the plate. Aunt Liza had fig preserves, blackberry jelly, and cane syrup. I had a hard time deciding, so I just took a little of each. She had also made red-eye gravy, and I had to have another biscuit to sop that up.

By the time I had eaten grits, eggs, bacon, ham, and biscuits chased down with buttermilk, I was stuffed.

Uncle Howard was too. He leaned back and patted his belly. "I'm as full as a tick on a hound dog's ear. Liza, you outdid yourself this morning."

I pushed back the cane-back chair and began to clear the table. Michael and Zeke both jumped up to help. I urged Aunt Liza to leave the cleaning with us, and she reluctantly complied.

I washed the dishes in the metal wash pan, Zeke dried, and Michael put them away. I couldn't help but think that this was the way it would be if Michael and I married.

Of course, I would have to learn to make biscuits as good as Aunt Liza's.

Michael placed the last dish on the shelf while I wiped off the red-checked tablecloth and wooden countertops. Uncle Howard had made the cabinets and painted them green with a floral design on the drawers between the white porcelain knobs. Had Uncle Howard painted the design or did Aunt Liza lend a hand? I would have to ask her.

I squeezed the water from the dish rag. When I took the pan of dirty dishwater out the backdoor, Zeke ran past me to play outside with the dogs.

When I came back in, Michael raked his hair back. His eyes were full of uncertainty, but his voice sounded confident. "Jay, I need to get going. I know you and Zeke will like it here." I felt a momentary panic, and Michael must have seen it. He wrapped his arms around me. "It'll be okay, my girl. I'll write, and you can write me. And I'll be back to see you in three shakes of a rooster's tail."

I pulled back so I could look into his face. "I wish you could stay, at least until school starts. I don't know anyone here, and Aunt Liza told me there are over four hundred students at the high school." I gave a little shudder.

"You'll make friends. And you have Zeke and your aunt and uncle."

"Yeah," I said, knowing I didn't have a clue how to make friends. Still, Aunt Liza and Uncle Howard were nice, and Aunt Liza was a great cook. And he was right. I had Zeke.

He cleared his throat and released me, half turning away. "Just send me a letter if you need me. I'll be here as fast as my old truck can make it."

"I'll write you as much as I can. But, I don't have any money for stamps. I hate to ask Aunt Liza."

He pulled a quarter from his pocket. "I wish I had more."

I wrapped his fingers around his money. "No, you keep it. You need it. The sooner you can save up enough, the sooner you can move here, and start college."

"It's just a quarter, Jay. You take it."

A quarter would buy a lot of stamps, but I shook my head. "No, it's a long ways home. You can stop and get a Coke."

He stuck the quarter back in his pocket and shook his head. "No, I won't be getting a Coke."

I grinned at him. "Without Zeke along, maybe you won't."

He laughed and went to check the oil in Mr. Drake's car. I pulled back the lace curtains and watched him from the window for a moment before going to tell Aunt Liza and Uncle Howard that he was leaving.

They followed me out. Zeke ran ahead of us and threw his arms around Michael's legs. Michael scooped him up to engulf him in a bear hug before setting him down.

Zeke looked at Michael with wide eyes. "I don't want you to go."

Michael mussed Zeke's hair. "I don't want to go, either, but sometimes we have to do what we don't want to." His eyes held mine for a second.

Zeke kicked the ground before tilting his head, the morning sun bathing his golden hair. "I wish Chance was here."

6

I wished we could have brought Chance, too. But we couldn't very well bring him in Mr. Drake's shiny car.

Uncle Howard gestured around the yard. "Son, we've got dogs aplenty for you to play with. And, if that's not enough, I'm sure we can find you another one." He laughed good naturedly.

Aunt Liza nodded her assent and gave Michael a hug. "We'll take good care of Jay and Zeke."

Michael shook Uncle Howard's hand and thanked him for everything.

Michael's eyes sought mine again. He held open his arms, and I walked into them. He squeezed me tight for a second. "Be good, my girl."

Words wouldn't pass the lump in my throat. He released me, and I stepped back as he climbed into the car.

I draped my arm over Zeke's shoulders, and we watched until the car was out of sight.

Chapter 2--Missing Michael

J moped around for a while, at a loss for anything to do. My aunt and uncle kept a few chickens, and Zeke and I went into the shed to get a small bucket of corn. The chickens were confined to a chicken coop, not like our chickens at home that ran loose in the yard.

Zeke scattered the feed on the ground while I held the bucket for him.

When I put the bucket back, Zeke pulled on my arm. "Jay, can we go see Uncle Howard?"

"I guess it'll be all right." I took his hand, and we walked the few feet to my uncle's shop.

The wood-working shop sprawled, untidily, behind the house. When I knocked, Uncle Howard called for us to come in.

His happiness shown as a beacon. "Come on in, young'ns."

"Wow." Zeke twirled around as he surveyed the tools, neatly hung on pegboards, and the half-finished projects that dotted the floor and benches.

A nearly finished table sat on the work surface in the middle. Uncle Howard pulled a stool up and patted it. "Zeke, want to help me?"

Zeke's eyes widened. "Can I?"

"You sure can."

I wandered away, while Uncle Howard bent his head close to Zeke's.

A baby cradle, covered in dust, dangled from the rafters in the back corner. Wooden boxes draped with a cloth stood beneath the cradle.

A few cane-back chairs leaned against the back wall with a doorway in the exact center. This led to a hall with rooms on each side. I went into the small room where Michael had slept last night and stared at the cot bumped up against the side wall.

Uncle Howard had told us he kept a couple of cots ready for homeless men that often came by. Although they had their own struggles, Aunt Liza and Uncle Howard still cared for those less fortunate.

Like us. Zeke and I were lucky to be here, I told myself. But, somehow, this morning, I didn't feel lucky. This wasn't home, was it? I missed my old house, my old life--not the part that had driven me here, but all the rest. But I couldn't go back--not now, anyway.

I went back to the main area and silently watched Uncle Howard and Zeke. Zeke was still young enough to adjust, to find a place here, by my uncle's side. But what of me?

Uncle Howard glanced at me and concern filled his eyes. "What's wrong, Jay?"

I shrugged my shoulders.

He got up and moved to me. "Jay, are you feeling homesick?"

"A little."

"I know it's a big change for you," he said.

I nodded my head. "I'm sorry, Uncle Howard." And, I truly was. Wasn't this better than on the farm working from dusk 'til dawn? Yet, I missed my home, missed Poppa, and, most of all, missed Michael. I tried to be thankful but failed miserably.

Uncle Howard rubbed his chin and looked from Zeke to me. "Did you two ever hear 'bout the frogs that fell into the churn?"

Zeke shook his head.

Uncle Howard drew another stool to his workbench and motioned for me to sit. He remained standing in front of us.

"Now let me see if I can recollect it." He hesitated another moment, still rubbing his chin, before beginning. "Two frogs hopped around one day and *kerplunk!* Would you believe both of them jumped right into a churn full of cream?" Here he paused while Zeke sucked air between his teeth. Uncle Howard suppressed a grin and continued. "One of the frogs just moaned and groaned. 'There's no way out,' he cried. The other, wiser, frog replied, 'I don't see a way out either, but, by gum, I'm going to keep trying.' But the first frog just wouldn't listen. He just plum felt sorry for himself. He quit swimming and sunk to the bottom of the churn. And, you know what happened to him?" He cocked an eyebrow at Zeke.

Zeke almost popped off his seat. "Did he drown, Uncle Howard?"

"Yes, siree, he drowned. But that wise frog, even though he felt sad for his friend, kept a swimming. 'Round and 'round he swam in that churn. And, guess what happened?"

Zeke's brow puckered. "What?"

I couldn't help but grin at Zeke's concern.

"That cream slowly changed into butter. The more that long-legged frog swam, the more butter formed. So much butter, the frog climbed right to the top of the churn and hopped out."

Zeke's eyes shone bright.

Uncle Howard looked directly at me. "Do you know the moral to the story, Jay?"

I straightened on the stool. "Yes, sir. Even when we're in a bad situation, we can't give up. We have to keep trying." *Easy words to say. Almost impossible to do when the pain of loss threatened to suffocate me.*

A look, almost of sorrow, clouded his eyes for a second before Uncle Howard nodded at Zeke. "Your sister's right. Now, you both need to just keep swimming. Don't ever give up."

"And things will get better? Will Momma get better?" Zeke asked.

"I'm sure she will, son. One way or t'other." Uncle Howard sat on his stool and picked up a piece of sand paper.

"Thanks, Uncle Howard, for the story." I got up and held out my hand for Zeke. "Come on. We've bothered Uncle Howard long enough."

Distress filled his eyes. "Can't I stay?" He glanced from me to Uncle Howard.

"Sure, you can. And you, too, Jay."

I shook my head. I wanted to get out into the fresh air, into the sunshine.

Uncle Howard waved a hand at me. "He'll be fine."

I smiled through my sadness. Zeke didn't need me. Again, I tried to shake off my depression. He loved me. Just because he wanted to spend time with Uncle Howard didn't mean he didn't love me.

Still, tears pricked my eyes when I left to walk down to the barn.

The ruts wound between a thick strand of pine trees. The grayed walls of the old barn suddenly loomed in front of me when I emerged from the pines.

Clothed In Thunder

Spider webs covered the building, inside and out. Empty stalls stood on each side along with a couple of padlocked rooms. Uncle Howard probably kept his tools in them. I walked down the center of the barn, batting away spider webs. With nothing to see, the dry, unused smell soon drove me back to the fresh air.

If the barn held life, pigs and cows like the barn at home, maybe it would ease the ache within. But, the farm was gone. And, this old barn held nothing of value.

Everything I loved, gone. I shook my head at myself. Not everything. I had Zeke. And Michael. And, Aunt Liza and Uncle Howard seemed nice enough, didn't they?

But my sadness refused to leave.

The dogs had followed me, and I spent a miserable hour or two throwing sticks for them, missing Chance more than ever. Slowly, I trailed back to the house. No Laurie, William, Aunt Jenny, or Uncle Colt. Loneliness engulfed me until I felt as if I were the frog drowning in the cream.

Fear of the new school churned and intermingled with my homesickness.

But hardest to endure was the missing of Michael, a physical pain that I knew not how to ease.

Chapter 3--New School

On Monday morning, we rose bright and early, and I dressed in my new clothes, admiring Aunt Liza's handiwork. She had made me two dresses and had bought me a pair of shoes, lace-up shoes with soles that didn't flap.

Zeke stayed home with Uncle Howard, while Aunt Liza and I walked the two blocks to the school. Stone steps led to double doors flanked by white columns.

On the threshold of the enormous, red-brick building, I smoothed my hair and took a deep breath.

My aunt entered first and turned to give me an encouraging smile. "Come on, Jay. You don't want to be late on your first day."

Clothed In Thunder

I stepped inside and blinked to adjust my eyes to the dimness. Aunt Liza hailed a student, a girl around my age. The girl smiled at me, revealing buck teeth. Yet, despite that, she was beautiful. Short, silvery blonde hair curled around her face, and serene blue eyes surveyed me. She pointed down the hall and nodded at something my aunt said.

My aunt took my arm, and we walked in the direction the girl had pointed. Before we rounded the corner, I turned to give the girl one last look.

The teeming students hurried orderly to their classes. The girl stood amidst them, as if in an oasis, and gave me a small wave. From this distance it looked as if concern furrowed her brow.

Near her was a male teacher. Shorter than most of the students and balding, yet still with a shock of black hair, he narrowed his dark eyes when his gaze fell on us. No wonder the girl looked concerned.

A sense of dread filled me that I tried to shake off. Clutching the tablet, pencil, and my syrup-can lunch pail so tightly to my chest that my knuckles whitened, I followed my aunt into the office.

She stood at the counter and fidgeted under the scrutiny of the secretary. "Miss Ballard, I wish to enroll my niece."

Was she nervous for me? I placed a hand on her arm to comfort both of us.

Miss Ballard gave a curt nod. "Yes, Mrs. Barnett. I heard your niece and nephew moved in with you." She pushed some papers across the counter. "What grade will she be entering?"

My aunt glanced at me, and I swallowed. Technically, I had never finished ninth grade. And now, also, I had missed the first two months of tenth grade.

I swallowed down the fear rising in my throat and raised my chin. "Tenth, Miss Ballard."

"Where did you last attend school?"

"Sterling School in Covington County." I looked down at my new pair of shoes. Sturdy brown leather whose soles didn't flap.

Miss Ballard handed a list to my aunt. "These are the books she'll need. The prices are beside each one."

My aunt's eyes widened. She shook her head as Miss Ballard came around the corner. "There aren't any cheaper books?"

"Oh, yes." Miss Ballard nodded vigorously. "You can get them used. As a matter of fact, I have some here you can choose from."

She walked to a cupboard and pulled down books in varying degrees of decrepitness. She pointed out the prices until my aunt cut her short.

"We'll take the cheapest ones." She glanced over at me, apologetically.

I gave her an encouraging smile. At least I had books for school, and that was all that mattered.

"I'll show you to your homeroom," Miss Ballard said. She stood by the door and waited.

Aunt Liza straightened my collar and gave my shoulder a squeeze. I gave her a quick hug, breathing in her smell of vanilla. I released her and followed Miss Ballard.

The empty hallways echoed the sounds of our clacking shoes. Sunlight streamed through the large windows but did little to dispel the gloom from the tall, dark, wood-beamed ceilings.

The hallway was eerily silent. For such a large school, the students seemed exceptionally quiet. Either that or the walls were thick enough to muffle all sounds.

She stopped at a door and turned to face me. "Sarah Jane, please let me know if, if . . ."

"Yes, Miss Ballard?"

She eyed me anxiously. Highly efficient until now, her sudden indecision worried me.

"Just let me know if you ever have a problem. Okay?"

"Yes, ma'am." What did she mean? A problem with a teacher or a student?

Before I had time to ask, she knocked briskly on the door.

"Your homeroom teacher is the geometry teacher, Mr. Albertson," she said as the door opened.

A girl held the door wide for us to enter. The room was filled with wall-to-wall students.

All eyes watched as the secretary ushered me to the front desk. Mr. Albertson pushed back his chair and stood.

My heart sank. The short, balding man.

His voice, when he spoke to Miss Ballard, reminded me of a crow cawing. His small, beady, black eyes under bushy brows darted from the secretary to me when she handed him the paper with my information, and he scowled.

Miss Ballard flashed me a smile although anxiety still clouded her eyes. She left, and Mr. Albertson eyed me without speaking. Then his gaze fell to the paper.

After a moment, he spoke. "Students, this is Sarah Jane Hunter." His eyes searched the room and landed on the girl who had held the door open. "Miss Sylvia, if you'd be so kind to see Miss Hunter doesn't get lost today."

Titters ran through the class. He nodded toward the back of the room. "Put your things in the cloak room, if you please, Miss Hunter."

Sylvia rose from her desk and accompanied me to the cloakroom. Hooks lined one wall with a wooden bench running the length of the wall beneath the hooks.

She pointed to an empty one. "That one can be yours."

"Thank you," I mumbled. I hung my sweater on the hook as she looked me up and down. I turned away, uncomfortable under her gaze, and placed my syrup can on the bench.

When I turned around, Sylvia had already left. I grabbed my books and hurried out.

Sylvia had settled back in her desk. Uncertain, I waited in the outer aisle, scanning the crowded room for an empty seat.

Mr. Albertson explained a problem at the blackboard, and his eyes flicked over me. He waved one hand toward the front of the room without pausing in his lecture.

I made my way slowly to the front, fully aware of the eyes of the students watching me. I stumbled over someone's outstretched leg, and one of my books fell to the floor. As I leaned over to pick it up, another book slid from my hands and slammed against the floor.

Mr. Albertson stopped speaking and turned fully to face me.

He pointed to the empty desk on the very front row. "Miss Hunter, will you please be seated?"

Again, titters ran through the class. Mr. Albertson picked up a wooden yardstick as I slid into my seat. He walked rapidly toward me and tapped my desk with the stick. When I jumped, the class erupted into full laughter.

Mr. Albertson banged the yardstick louder. "Quiet!" He took a step back and glowered at the class.

I hugged the books to my chest and sat with my back rigid. The laughter petered out, and I carefully raised the lid a few inches and slipped the books in.

"Miss Hunter!"

The lid slid from my fingers and clattered down.

"Geometry book? Pencil? Paper?" He was leaning over, only inches from my face. Once again he hit my desk before moving away.

I threw the lid open and clawed through the books, searching for the geometry book. Panic seized me when I realized I didn't have one.

Mr. Albertson picked up the chalk and explained the problem. I lowered the lid and raised my hand.

When Mr. Albertson saw me, he sighed deeply. "Yes, Miss Hunter?"

"I can't find my book, sir." I bit my bottom lip.

He strode to my desk and flung the lid open. I leaned as far away from him as possible but still caught his smell, a combination of stale air and mothballs. He rummaged through the desk, slamming it shut after a minute.

"You are correct, Miss Hunter. Please go back to the office and purchase one."

My thoughts raced. I didn't have any money. Would they loan me a book?

"Now, Miss Hunter!" The pitch of his voice rose, making him sound more than ever like a crow.

I jumped from my seat and scurried to the door. I pulled the door shut behind me and waited a moment, steadying my breathing.

I peered up and down the hallway. Which way was the office? Why hadn't I paid attention? All the doors looked the same, the same darkened wood as the ceilings. Grayish-beige paint adorned all the walls.

I shifted from one foot to another. I knew I couldn't stand here all day. I finally made a decision and headed right. Then, a hallway led to the left, and I started down it.

After only a minute or two, I realized my mistake. This way led deeper into the building. The office had been at the front.

I retraced my steps. I would simply have to go back to class and tell Mr. Albertson.

But when I reached the original hallway, I didn't know which door led to his class. The only means to distinguish one from another were the metal numbers hanging on the doorframe. Why hadn't I paid attention to the number?

I sighed and started in another direction, searching for anything that looked familiar. Two boys walked twenty or so feet ahead of me, and I hurried to catch them. They entered a door with a metal sign that said "Boys" before I reached them.

Clothed In Thunder

My shoulders slumped in defeat. I heard steps behind me, and fear knotted in my stomach. I clenched my fists, digging my nails into my palms, and turned to face the person.

Chapter 4--Making a Friend

The girl who had pointed Aunt Liza and me in the direction of the office smiled at me. The one with the pale blonde hair and the bluest eyes I had ever seen. They made my little brother's eyes look dull in comparison.

She smiled at me shyly, revealing her only flaw, the buck teeth.

"Are you lost?" she asked in a voice as soft as a feather.

I nodded unhappily. "I'm looking for the office."

"Yes, I know. I'm in your geometry class. My name's Marla."

She spoke so warmly that I had to smile back. "It's nice to meet you. Everyone calls me Jay."

"Mr. Albertson sent me to find you. I'll show you the office." She turned, and I put out my hand to stop her.

"Marla . . ." I swallowed and warmth flooded my face.

"Yes, Jay?" She gave me her full attention.

"I don't have any money to pay for the book." I ducked my head and sighed.

When I glanced up, she was staring out the window. Then she nodded and faced me. "We could share a book."

I straightened and searched her serene face. "Really? Will Mr. Albertson allow it?"

"I don't know. We don't have to tell him." She continued surveying me with her unclouded blue eyes.

I shrugged my shoulders. "I guess it wouldn't hurt. We can try it for a while until I can get the money."

Marla glanced at the watch she wore. "Class is almost over. We need to hurry." She spun on her heel and walked quickly down the hallway.

I followed, struggling to keep up with her long-legged stride. The bell rang. Doors opened and students streamed out. We fought against the stream, dodging elbows and the books students carried by straps slung over shoulders.

We reached the classroom as other students came in.

"You need your English and history books," Marla said.

I grabbed my books and rushed from the room, searching for Marla. She spotted me first and called my name. She beckoned for me to follow her. The hall was almost empty, and I hurried to catch up with her.

We arrived at our next class, out of breath. The teacher had her hand on the door, ready to close it.

"Miss Weaver, this is a new student, Sarah Jane Hunter." Marla left us.

Miss Weaver's smile revealed evenly spaced, sparkling white teeth. Auburn hair cascaded around her shoulders making her beautiful.

"Which do you prefer? Sarah or Jane?"

My tense muscles relaxed in her welcoming presence. "I actually prefer Jay." I followed her into the classroom.

Even though the students all sat at attention, she clapped twice and placed a hand on my shoulder. "Class, this is a new student, Jay. Please give her a warm welcome."

Acutely aware of the curious stares of the students, I followed Miss Weaver to an empty desk, almost at the back of the room.

She patted my back before stepping to the front. She sat down behind a large wooden desk and pulled a leather-bound notebook to her. She ran a slim finger down the page. "Today four students will be giving speeches. Andrew Mathison is first."

A slim boy, with a head of hair sticking up in odd places and a sprinkling of freckles, walked to the front of the room. His hands shook slightly.

Miss Weaver smiled reassuringly at him. "Andrew, just release your ego."

A look of puzzlement crossed his face. "I ain't got an eagle, Miss Weaver."

"*I don't have an eagle*," she corrected.

"Me, neither." He scratched his head.

Miss Weaver's face twitched as if she tried to suppress a smile. "Not eagle. *Ego.*"

"Ego?"

"Yes. Ego is 'self.' Don't think about self. Think about your fellow students and conveying information to them. You're not doing this for yourself."

"Not for myself?" His look of bewilderment increased. "We ain't getting graded?"

"*We're not*, Andrew," she corrected again.

"Whew, that's a relief."

The class laughed, and Miss Weaver chuckled with them.

When the laughter died down, Miss Weaver tried again. "Andrew, you *are* getting graded. Now, no more *ain'ts*."

He looked down at the paper in his hand. "My report ain't about ants."

The classroom erupted in laughter, and Miss Weaver shushed them. "Andrew! 'Ain't' is incorrect grammar. You know that."

"Yes, ma'am. Reckon I just forgot." He grinned at her.

She smiled back and motioned for him to proceed.

Maybe this school wouldn't be so bad after all. I settled back in my seat and let my mind drift. I wondered how Momma was doing and if she missed me and Zeke.

I missed Poppa so much! Sometimes it just didn't seem real that he had died. But he had, and Zeke and I would just have to make a new life here with Aunt Liza. She and Uncle Howard had been so good to us already. Still, I missed Poppa, the farm, and Michael. I daydreamed of Michael, of what it would be like when we married. Would we move back home, to the farm? Or, would we live here in town?

Then something wet and squishy hit the side of my face. *A spit ball.*

I cringed. *Not another Dan Drake!* I looked around, and no one seemed a likely culprit. There were no mean-looking boys sitting near me. Only Sylvia and three other girls. They all seemed absorbed in the slim boy's report.

The spitball lay on my desk as evidence that I didn't imagine it. I shrugged my shoulders and did as the four girls were doing. I folded my hands, crossed my ankles, and listened attentively to the rest of the reports.

At the end of class, Sylvia walked over to me, sweeping her thick wavy hair away from her face. "History is next. Do you have your history book?"

The three girls gathered around us as I held mine up. One of the girls snickered when she saw its tattered cover. I hastily grabbed the tablet from my desk and slipped it on top.

Another of the girls whispered to Sylvia, holding her hand so that I couldn't read her lips.

Sylvia grinned and nodded her head before she gestured to me. "Come on."

She headed from the room without waiting for a reply, her three friends jostling for a position by her side. Walking behind them, I noticed they all wore light-colored stockings, all except one girl. She didn't have on stockings at all but wore a pair of socks folded over at the ankles. I had never seen a girl with bare legs before, leastways, not in public. My stockings were thick and dark. My shoes laced up.

None of them wore laced-up shoes. Their shoes had straps that buckled. I noticed their clothes for the first time—skirts and pull-over sweaters. And all had bobbed hair with varying degrees of waves and curls.

My eyes swept the hall, and I saw two or three other girls dressed like me--long hair, dresses instead of skirts, and dark stockings. They walked with their heads down, not laughing and joking like the four girls in front of me.

I scoffed. What did hair and clothes matter anyhow? It didn't matter if someone dressed richly or poorly, we were to treat everyone the same. If Sylvia and her friends didn't know that, well . . . they just weren't raised right.

When we reached the classroom, I looked for Marla. She, too, wore the light-colored stockings and the buckled shoes. Yet, she sat alone. If no one liked her, it wasn't because of her clothes or hair.

The history teacher gave me a seat next to Marla. I dismissed Sylvia and her friends from my mind. I would stick with Marla.

Chapter 5--Dan

The rest of the day dragged, and I was yawning when I walked down the cement steps after the last bell. Glad to be leaving the gloom of the building, I paused as my eyes adjusted to the sun's slanting rays.

Someone called my name and the voice sounded familiar. *Surely it couldn't be.* My eyes searched the area.

My mouth fell open, and I blinked, not believing what I saw.

Dan Drake!

He wore an army uniform and leaned against the Phaeton, his arms folded.

Clothed In Thunder

I simply stared for a second while he straightened and took a step toward me.

"What are you doing here?" I finally managed.

"Hello to you, too." He chuckled softly. "I've finished up basic training and had a three-week furlough. I thought I'd stop by and say hi."

Was he serious? He came all the way to Plainsville and looked me up just to say hi? "Well, hi. Umm . . . I got to head home."

"Can I give you a ride?"

I looked at the Phaeton. I wasn't the only one checking it out. A crowd had gathered around, including Sylvia and her friends. A couple of boys were kicking at the wheels, and Dan moved away from me to pop the hood.

Sylvia sidled over to me. "Who's your friend, Sarah Jane?"

That was the first time she had called me by name. I smiled. Dan Drake and Sylvia were made for each other. "Oh, Dan . . ."

"Yes?" He peered around the cover of the hood.

"I'd like you to meet someone. This is Sylvia. Sylvia, Dan Drake."

"I just love your car!" She widened her eyes and tilted her head to one side, allowing a lock of hair to brush her cheek.

Dan barely looked at her. Disappointment washed over me. Never had two people deserved each other more.

Dan closed the hood and walked back to me. "Jay, do your friends need a ride?"

"Oh," Sylvia said, before I could reply. "That would be wonderful. Thank you so much, Dan." She reached out to touch his arm.

I shrugged my shoulders. "Have fun. I've got to be getting home." I started to move away.

"Jay, you, too!" Dan held the door open for me and gestured.

I longed to ride in the car. Why not? It was only a ride. Nothing big. I hesitated one more second, climbed in, and murmured a thank you.

Sylvia ducked her head to look at me. "Sarah Jane, please slide over. I'm going to sit up here. May Lou, Darcy, and Wren are going to sit in the back."

Why hadn't I allowed Sylvia in first? Gritting my teeth, I slid toward the middle and scrunched up. Dan closed the doors for Sylvia and the giggling girls.

Sylvia whispered in my ear. "He's so handsome!"

Handsome? *Dan?* He crawled in, and I squeezed my arms together, so no part of my body would touch him.

Still, his arm brushed against mine when he started the car. I eyed him surreptitiously. Why would Sylvia think he was good looking? I tried to see him objectively. In the uniform, he did look better. He was clean shaven and healthy looking. The army had been good for him.

But he was still Dan! I drew myself in tighter as he glanced around.

"Where to, ladies?" he asked.

I spoke up quickly. "Go straight here and turn to the second right."

Why had I gotten into this car? The pleasure of the drive wasn't worth the agony of sitting between Dan and Sylvia.

When Dan's eyes fell on me, the girls in the back giggled.

"How was school today?"

"Fine," I answered.

The giggling in the back grew louder, and Sylvia shook her head at them.

"Fine," I repeated emphatically. "How did you do in basic?"

"Fine," he mimicked. He flashed a smile.

For the first time I noticed he had dimples, and fine laugh lines framed his eyes.

"Do you mind if I drop by later today?" he asked.

I ignored his question. "That next house is where I'm living."

Why did he want to come over? What was he doing here? Did he have news about Momma or Michael?

He had the car, so he'd obviously been home. Maybe he wanted to tell me something. Something about Michael? Did he have a message from him?

"Well?" He cast another glance at me.

I nodded. "Come over about seven."

Dan brought the car to a stop and jumped out. I would have opened the door myself, but Sylvia just sat there and waited until he opened it for her.

"You are so kind," she said to him as she gracefully exited the car.

I climbed out, mumbled my thanks, and rushed away, peals of laughter from the back seat following me.

In the kitchen, Aunt Liza was alone, peeling potatoes.

"Where's Zeke?" I asked.

"He's gone to town with Howard. He follows him everywhere he goes." Her eyes brightened.

I retrieved a knife and bowl, sat down, and reached for a potato.

"Anything wrong?" she asked. "You look flushed."

I cut the potato into small cubes. "Someone was waiting for me after school today."

She looked at me curiously. "Who?"

"Dan Drake. I think I told you about him."

"He's the one whose horse broke William's leg. Colt wrote me a letter when it happened."

"Yes, ma'am. That was my fault." I squirmed at the memory, wondering if Uncle Colt blamed me. "Anyway, he wants to come over. If it's okay with you and Uncle Howard?"

"It's okay with us if it's okay with you. Whatever you want."

Clothed In Thunder

I dropped a potato peeling on the linoleum floor and bent to pick it up. "I don't want him to come over. I thought maybe he had a message from Michael. Or maybe Momma."

She nodded her head. "Could be." She took the bowl and knife from my hands. "You go on and do your homework. I'll finish up supper."

"Yes, ma'am." I gathered my books and paused. "Aunt Liza, did you pay for a math book? I couldn't find it."

She looked embarrassed. "I didn't have enough money. I meant to tell you this morning but forgot. We can borrow some money. . ."

I quickly shook my head. "The girl from this morning--Marla, do you know her?"

She nodded. "Yes, I know her family well."

"She told me I could share her book."

Aunt Liza looked relieved. "Okay, then. Maybe in a few days, we can get you one."

"Yes, ma'am." I went to my room and sat down on the bed. What in the world did Dan want?

No need fretting over it. I'd know soon enough.

Chapter 6--The Visit

Zeke and I were helping Aunt Liza with the last of the dishes when we heard a car and the dogs barking. I left Aunt Liza and Zeke in the kitchen.

Uncle Howard, already at the front door, ushered Dan in.

"Hi," I mumbled.

Aunt Liza came out of the kitchen, and I introduced Dan to her and Uncle Howard.

Aunt Liza gestured at the couch. "Come on in and sit a spell. Would you like a glass of tea?"

"Yes, ma'am. Thank you." Dan took a seat on the couch.

Zeke peeked out from behind Uncle Howard's chair.

"Hi, Zeke." Dan grinned and motioned at my brother. "What's that in your ear?"

Zeke approached him cautiously, feeling the ear Dan had pointed to. "Nothing."

Dan pulled Zeke closer to him. "Let me see." After a few grunting sounds, Dan pretended to extract a quarter from his ear. "There you go, little buddy. You're growing quarters."

"I am?" Zeke's eyes widened. "Is this mine?" He took the quarter from Dan, turning it over and over.

"You grew it, didn't you?" Dan smiled at Zeke.

Uncle Howard laughed as Zeke jumped up and down. He turned his other ear to Dan. "Are there any more?"

I couldn't help but grin at Zeke. "It takes a long time for a quarter to grow. That's a lot of money."

Zeke crawled up beside Dan, still examining his quarter.

"How's the army treating you, son?" Uncle Howard asked.

"Not bad. Three square meals a day." He looked at me with a hint of shyness. "The army has a program that allows drop outs to get their high school diploma. I should have mine in a couple of months."

I cleared my throat and attempted a smile. "That's great, Dan."

Aunt Liza returned with a tray of glasses filled with iced tea. I jumped up to help her at the same time Dan did, and our shoulders brushed.

I stepped back as he handed out the glasses. Aunt Liza thanked him profusely, and we all settled down with our tea.

I'd never had iced tea until I moved in with Aunt Liza and Uncle Howard. The iceman brought a block of ice every week for their icebox, and Aunt Liza would shave off slivers of ice for the tea.

"This is delicious," Dan said, smiling at Aunt Liza.

"So, how long are you going to be in town?" she asked.

"Just today in Plainsville. I'm going down home tonight. I have a three-week furlough and plan to spend it with my father on the farm." He glanced in my direction. "I'm stationed just north of here, about forty minutes away. Plainsville is on my way back to camp, and I'd like to stop by again."

To see me? I frowned. Why this sudden change? I stood up, suddenly feeling stifled. "I'll be back in a minute," I mumbled, not waiting for a response.

The cool October air hit my cheeks as I went out. The cedar tree in the backyard beckoned. Its fragrance comforted me as I drew near.

Clothed In Thunder

Darkness had gathered quickly, and the moon had risen. The cedar basked in its light.

I was being rude, leaving so abruptly. *But it was only Dan.* Who cared what he thought? I sighed deeply, feeling sorry for myself. I had enough problems without Dan coming here.

Immediately I felt ashamed. God had blessed me richly, and I should be thankful. I had a roof over my head, food to fill me, shoes that didn't flap, iced tea, my family. And Michael.

A warmth filled me thinking of him. Had it only been a few days since I had last seen him? It felt like an eternity.

Minutes ticked by as I looked into the night sky, picking out constellations in the velvety blackness. The black sky looked like a shadow, a reassuring presence, like a thick quilt I could snuggle into.

The *comfort* I knew when Poppa had still been alive. But I had Michael now. He helped fill the void.

I lingered, listening to the sounds of the night, counting my blessings, and thinking of Michael.

When the backdoor squeaked open, I straightened and watched as Dan approached.

I didn't move from my spot. He came and stopped in front of me without speaking.

"What are you doing here, Dan?" I strove to keep my voice level, unemotional.

"Your aunt sent me to find you."

I sighed deeply. "That's not what I meant. Why did you come to see me? Do you have news from Michael? Or, Momma?"

He shook his head. "That's not why I'm here. Jay . . ." His eyes shone in the moonlight and held mine. His voice became husky. "I've learned a lot the last few months. And I've been doing a lot of thinking. I wanted to apologize for all I put you through." His hand closed gently over my wrist. "You and your family."

I stepped back, pulling my wrist from his grasp. "There was no need to come here to apologize. You could have written me a letter."

He moved toward me, and his voice rose. "I had to tell you that I was drunk when my horse broke William's leg. And when I threw the snowball at the horse." He shook his head. "I was drunk most of the time. But I've sobered up now. I had to let you know."

"Drunk?" I puckered my brow.

"I was young and foolish. And weak. I'm sorry for hurting William, for almost hurting you when Blaze bucked you off."

I half-turned away, and he took my arm again and pulled me to him.

"Jay, won't you let me apologize?" His voice softened and fell to a whisper.

"Apology accepted. Please let go of me." I looked down at his hand on my arm, and he released me.

Clothed In Thunder

I spun around and bounded up the steps of the back porch. Breathing hard, I entered the sitting room.

Aunt Liza looked at me in alarm. "Are you okay, Jay?"

I nodded and flopped down on the couch by Uncle Howard. Zeke climbed into my lap, still holding the quarter.

Dan came in and picked up his cap from the table. "I'd best be going." He didn't look at me.

"Nice meeting you, son," Uncle Howard said, standing to shake his hand.

Aunt Liza walked with him to the door. "Come back to see us."

I shot her a hard look and shook my head slightly. She frowned at me. Uncle Howard, Aunt Liza, and Zeke followed Dan outside. I stayed where I was on the couch.

I picked up my glass and pressed its coolness against my hot forehead.

When they came back in, Aunt Liza had a smile playing around her lips.

"Such a nice young man!" She stopped in front of me. "Jay, you were rude to Dan, running out like that."

"Sorry," I mumbled.

"He's bringing his horses next Friday for us to board, and he's going to spend the weekend," Uncle Howard said.

My mouth flew open. "No! Not here!"

Uncle Howard sat down beside me. "Jay, I'm surprised at you! His father doesn't have time to exercise the horses, and Dan asked me to board them here."

I shook my head vehemently.

"Jay, he's paying me to board the horses. It's not much, but every little bit helps. Besides, he thought you would like having horses that you could ride when you wanted."

I shook my head. "No, I don't want him coming back here."

Aunt Liza pressed her lips firmly together and gave me a long, hard stare. "Jay, this is our house, and we can invite anyone we want."

My cheeks burned, and my gaze dropped to my hands clasped tightly in my lap. Here Zeke and I were being a financial burden, and all I could do was complain. "I'm sorry. I had no right to say that." I squirmed uneasily. "You just don't know what Dan has done."

"He told us some things while you were outside."

Zeke piped up. "He seems a lot nicer now, Jay."

Aunt Liza bestowed a smile on Zeke before turning back to me. "People can change. Even if he hasn't changed, you still need to treat him kindly."

My cheeks burned hotter. "Yes, ma'am."

Clothed In Thunder

I helped carry the glasses into the kitchen. Maybe he was simply coming back to bring his horses.

Maybe even to see Sylvia.

I could only hope.

Chapter 7--The Punishment

The next day, I left for school by myself. I enjoyed the walk in the coolness of the fall morning. Some of the leaves were finally beginning to turn. The leaves of the oak trees, browned as if left in the oven too long, interspersed with leaves of blazing yellow from hickory nut trees. Dreading the gloom of the school, I dragged my feet up the steps of stone.

I twisted my mouth into a smile before entering the building with the other students. I didn't see anyone I recognized from yesterday but managed to find my homeroom. After yesterday's experience, I made sure I had at least memorized the class number.

Clothed In Thunder

I waited until the cloakroom emptied, before I hung up my sweater and put my lunch, still in the syrup can, on the bench. When I turned around, Marla walked in.

Her face lit up. "Good morning, Jay."

"Hi."

. Before I could say another word, I heard Mr. Albertson tapping his desk with the yardstick. I scurried to my assigned seat. As soon as everyone had settled down, Mr. Albertson told us to get out our homework. He then walked around the room, beginning in the back, to pick up the work. Mine was the last desk he stopped at.

"Where is your homework, Miss Hunter?"

I glanced at him briefly before lowering my eyes. "Sir, I wasn't in class when you assigned the work."

He walked to his desk and laid the homework papers down, placing a large iron paperweight on top. He picked up a ruler and returned to my desk.

"I wrote the homework on the board before class. It was your responsibility to make sure you received the assignment." He slapped the ruler against his thigh. "Hold out your hand."

I hesitated before I held my arm out.

"Palm up, Miss Hunter."

I twisted my wrist to expose my palm. He grasped my fingers, pulling them back. He then whacked my palm three times.

I took the punishment in silence, but the pain made tears stand in my eyes. I willed the tears not to roll down my cheeks, angry at the injustice.

After a long, cold stare, he marched to the blackboard and explained the day's work.

I hunched over my paper, writing down everything he said with my stinging right hand. Why hadn't I held out my left? Next time I would.

I shook my head. There wouldn't be a next time.

I hoped.

At lunch, I didn't seek out Marla. Instead, I slunk to an empty spot near the wall. I didn't look up until someone spoke. Marla's clear blue eyes surveyed me solemnly as she perched on the edge of her seat.

She reached across the table to pat my arm. "I'm sorry, Jay."

"No need to be."

I'd been through worse but didn't tell her, not wanting her pity. *This was nothing compared to the pain of that.*

I shrugged my shoulders.

She smiled at me reassuringly. "Why don't you come over to my house after school, and I can help you with your homework?"

"Thanks. That sounds swell." I clamped a hand over my mouth.

"What's wrong?" Marla watched me, curiosity brimming in her eyes.

I laughed. "I've never said swell before. I'm already sounding like people around here."

"Well, you sure don't look like anyone around here." This time Marla clamped a hand to her mouth. Laughter leaked out. "I didn't mean that like it sounded. I mean with your dark hair and blue eyes."

I smiled wryly. "That's okay, Marla. I know I look like a country hick."

"Oh, Jay!" Distress shone in her eyes.

"Really. It's okay. People can think what they want."

She beamed at me. "What a great attitude. It's one I try to have."

And we both giggled, why I didn't know. It was the first time I ever remembered giggling with anyone.

What did it matter what others thought, if I could at least have one friend? And, Marla, for whatever reason, seemed to be willing to be friends.

We left the lunchroom side by side.

I stepped outside that afternoon, intent on hurrying home to tell Aunt Liza I would be going to Marla's. When someone called my name, I relived yesterday. A vehicle was parked in the exact spot where Dan's car had been, and a young man leaned against it.

He pushed away from the truck and hurried toward me. I blinked my eyes and ran down the steps to meet him.

Michael! He caught me in his arms, and it was all I could do to step back, aware that teachers patrolled nearby.

"Michael! What are you doing here?"

"I couldn't wait another minute to see you." His eyes held mine, and he sighed heavily. "But I've got to head back tonight."

I heard peals of laughter. Again, it was Sylvia and her friends. I was thankful Michael drove an old truck, and Sylvia wouldn't be able to wedge her way in.

Still, the girls gathered around us and forced me to introduce them. This time, they only stayed a minute before moving away. I prayed my thanks and climbed in beside Michael.

His hand reached for mine. "Where to, my girl?"

"I need to stop by the house, and then I'm going to a friend's." I threaded my fingers through his and bit my bottom lip.

He looked at me, concern in his eyes. "What's wrong?"

I explained to him about Mr. Albertson.

He shook his head. "That's just ridiculous. That man needs talking to. Why would anyone act like that?"

"I just hate that you came all this way, and I have to do homework." I looked at him anxiously, half afraid he would be angry with me.

"It would be worth driving twice as long just to spend one second with you." He squeezed my hand, and my heart melted.

"When can you come back to spend longer?"

"I'll try to make it back this weekend. Working overtime, trying to make enough money to pay for college, and helping my paw around the farm, makes it hard to get away."

We pulled into the yard, and I jumped out to tell Aunt Liza that I would be at Marla's and that Michael was driving me.

When I came back, Michael's face lit up.

"Aunt Liza told me to invite you to supper." I looked at him, my fingers crossed.

"What is she cooking?"

I gently punched his arm. "Michael! I thought you wanted to see me."

"I do! I'll eat pork liver for you." He threw me a sideways glance. "But I hope it's not pork liver."

"It's pork chops."

"Great! I'm definitely staying, then." He flashed a smile. "But I'll have to leave right after supper."

"Are you sure? You can't stay longer?"

"Girl, you don't know how much I want to." He turned down a side road and threw the truck into park.

He gathered me to him, and I leaned into his kiss, not wanting to ever let him go.

But thoughts of Mr. Albertson intruded, and I reluctantly pulled away. "Marla will wonder where I'm at."

"You're right. I don't want to keep you from your homework."

A scent drifted from Michael. "What's that smell?"

"What smell?" He looked at me, frowning.

"Are you wearing cologne?"

He smiled. "Yep. Just for you." He grinned lopsidedly.

I kissed him gently on the lips before he drove me to Marla's. He dropped me off with a promise to meet me back at Aunt Liza's for supper.

Chapter 8--Marla

Marla lived in a comfortable two-story house. A sitting room, formal parlor, a bedroom, and a kitchen made up the downstairs. Upstairs were three more bedrooms where Marla and her four brothers and three sisters slept.

A cold front had moved through, and the temperature hovered already at freezing, making Marla's bedroom too cool to study in. Instead, we settled at the kitchen table, the warmth from the stove filling the room. Marla sat beside me, and her youngest brothers and sisters gathered around us, clamoring for our attention.

Marla's mother, a tired-looking woman, shooed the children, all except the youngest girl, into the sitting room, leaving us to a relative peace.

The sounds of laughter drifted through the walls. What would it be like to be part of such a large family? I would never know.

"This is Grace," Marla said, wrapping her arm around the young girl by her side.

"Hi, Grace. How old are you?" I asked.

"Eight." She moved even closer to Marla and stared at me.

"Grace, don't you want to go play with the others?" Marla asked.

Grace shook her head, sending her golden curls swaying. If possible, her beauty outshone her sister's.

"We have to study," Marla said. "You have to be very quiet."

Grace nodded her head without speaking. She settled with her arms folded on the table, resting her head on them.

Marla didn't waste any more time but opened the math book and showed me the problems. I couldn't make hide nor hair of them. Without losing patience, she flipped to the front of the book and patiently explained the very first lesson. I had missed so much school that it took a while to understand even the basic principles.

Marla never complained at my slowness. With her encouragement, I began to catch on.

Clothed In Thunder

After two hours, we had covered the first three chapters. But it was too little, too late. The class was now in the middle of chapter eight. No way I could do my homework for tomorrow when there was so much more to learn.

Nothing I could do but leave with my homework undone. I shoved my uneasiness aside, knowing I would just have to wait for the morrow. Maybe Mr. Albertson would understand. Yet, I knew it was a foolish thought.

I thanked Marla quietly. Grace slept, snoring softly, and I didn't want to wake her. I gathered my books and hurried home.

Aunt Liza had made mashed potatoes, turnips, and cornbread to go along with the fried pork chops. It was a perfect meal with Michael sitting by my side.

As we finished up with a sweet potato cobbler, I repeated the story of Mr. Albertson.

Aunt Liza sucked air between her teeth. "I can't believe he holds a grudge after all these years!" Her face reddened.

I looked at her in surprise. "You know Mr. Albertson?"

She nodded and took a bite of the cobbler. My spoon remained dangling in my hand even though sweet potato cobbler was my favorite dessert.

Uncle Howard shook his head at his wife. "Might as well tell them, Liza."

She swallowed the bite of cobbler and toyed with the rest in her plate before she spoke. "We graduated from high school together. He was valedictorian, and I was salutatorian."

"You look a lot younger than he does," I said.

"Thank you, hon." She bestowed a smile on me. "Anyway, we both had to give speeches at graduation. I stole the one he had written." She shrugged her shoulders.

It was hard for me to imagine Aunt Liza doing that. "He knew you stole it?"

She nodded her head. "Yes, he knew, but no one else. He never told." She looked down at her plate, her cheeks red.

"Well, I'm sure he deserved it," Michael said.

Aunt Liza raised her head, and her eyes clouded. She shook her head. "No, he didn't deserve it. I was just. . . jealous."

"Did he give the speech?" I asked.

She waved her hand. "Oh, sure. Our English teacher helped him rewrite it. He remembered most of it, anyway."

"Well, I think he's plum silly to be mad all these years." I rubbed my forehead. "Maybe he's still not mad--he just doesn't like me."

Aunt Liza shook her finger at me. "Now you're just being silly. Why wouldn't he like you?"

I shrugged my shoulders.

Michael pushed back from the table. "Sorry to eat and run, but I need to get going."

I sighed. "I still have English and history homework to do."

"Go, go," Aunt Liza said. "I'll do the dishes."

"Can I help?" Zeke asked.

"You sure can. You want to wash or dry?"

I walked out with Michael. The air was cool, and I shivered. We stood by his truck with flaking red paint, showing rust beneath. I thought how it contrasted with Dan's shiny car.

I turned to Michael. "I forgot to tell you. Dan came by."

"He didn't tell me when I saw him." Michael frowned. "What did he want?"

I shrugged my shoulders. "I don't know, except he said he wanted to apologize."

Michael rubbed his chin. "Yeah. He's been doing a lot of apologizing."

"He apologized to you, too?"

Michael nodded slowly. "Reckon you could say that."

"Oh, and he's coming back this weekend. He's bringing horses for Uncle Howard to board."

Michael's eyebrows drew together. "He told me he needed my help but didn't say why. Guess he wants to borrow me and my truck." He kissed my forehead, and I caught the scent of his new cologne.

"Be careful going home."

"See you Friday, if the creeks don't rise."

I smiled, and he drove away. I went to my bedroom to finish my homework, already missing him.

Chapter 9--The Office Visit

The next morning rain clouds had gathered. When I was still a block away from school, the rain began. I was soaked when I entered the building and made my way through the crowded halls. Thunder shook the glass in the windows.

I shivered as I waited for Mr. Albertson to pick up the homework. The thunder rumbled farther away, but the clouds still hung dark and heavy. The lights did little to dispel the gloom.

Mr. Albertson made his way around the room until he once again stopped at my desk. "Homework, Miss Hunter?" His voice sounded more than ever like the cawing of a crow.

I looked down at my desk. "I'm sorry, sir."

"What is your excuse today?" He crossed his arms, and his face took on the contortions of someone eating an unripe persimmon.

"I didn't know how," I said. "Marla went over the first three chapters with me, but that was as far as we got."

He cast Marla a malevolent stare as if she had betrayed him before turning his anger back to me. "Stand up, Miss Hunter."

I hastily obeyed. The class started to snicker, but one look threw them into silence.

"To the blackboard."

I walked to the board. My hands trembled slightly, and I rubbed my nose to hide my nervousness.

Mr. Albertson thrust a piece of chalk at me. "Let's see exactly how much you do know."

My cheeks burned as he wrote a series of problems across the board. He spun to face me and narrowed his eyes.

"You may begin." A thin strand of his remaining dark hair fell over one eye as he jerked his head at me.

The board wavered before my eyes, and I squinted as if that would help. My stomach churned as I attempted the first one. I swallowed hard and moved to the next one. I had no clue how to proceed. Several students giggled. I gulped the air, trying desperately to calm myself.

Finally, I squared my shoulders and turned to face him. "I can't do any more, sir."

He kept his eyes on me and spat out a command. "Miss Sylvia, up front, now."

Sylvia walked regally to the front of the room. "Yes, sir?"

"You're in charge while I'm gone."

Quickly, he grabbed my elbow and propelled me toward the door. I was barely able to keep pace with him, even as short as he was. By the time we reached the office, I was out of breath.

He released my arm and banged on the counter, startling Miss Ballard.

She jumped from her chair. "Mr. Albertson! Anything wrong?"

He ignored her question. "Where is Principal Martin?"

"He's in his office. I'll tell him you're here." She threw a look of sympathy at me before going into the inner office.

She returned in a few seconds. "He can see you now."

Mr. Albertson pushed me forward. My heart pounded in my ears. What would Mr. Martin do? Would I be kicked out of school for not doing my homework?

Anger surged, and my head throbbed. I straightened to my full height and marched ahead of Mr. Albertson. I pushed the anger away and moistened my lips.

Principal Martin stood as we entered. Mr. Albertson explained the situation.

I studied the many books on the bookshelves lining the walls, trying to distract myself as Mr. Albertson hurled accusations at me.

The principal walked to the front of the desk and leaned against it, studying me. I turned my full attention to him.

"Miss Hunter, did we make a mistake placing you in tenth grade?"

"No, sir," I said, firmly. "I know I can do the work if I have time to catch up."

Mr. Albertson snorted. "I will not have a student in my classroom who refuses to do homework. She doesn't even try."

I stared down at my shoes, biting my lip to keep from blurting out.

"Do you refuse to do your homework?" Principal Martin asked.

I raised my head to meet his eyes. "No, sir. Marla helped me to learn the first three chapters. We didn't have time to do more."

"Mr. Albertson, did you examine her on those chapters?"

"No, sir, but . . ."

Principal Martin waved his hand in dismissal. "Give her until Monday. If she's not caught up by then, we'll see what other arrangements need to be made."

Mr. Albertson gritted his teeth and glared at me.

I swallowed. "Principal Martin?"

"Yes, Miss Hunter?" He had moved back around his desk.

"I don't have a math book. I live with my aunt and uncle, and they couldn't afford all of my books."

He sighed. "Mr. Barnett is your uncle?"

"Yes, sir."

He studied me for a long minute before sighing. "Times are hard for everyone. Mr. Albertson, do you have an extra textbook in your room Miss Hunter may borrow?"

Mr. Albertson threw back his shoulders. "I'm not sure if she should be trusted with one of our books." He threw me a look of distaste.

Mr. Martin shook his head slowly at him and wagged his index finger. "We will trust her with the book until the time she shows herself untrustworthy."

Mr. Albertson stiffened. "If you say so, sir."

I nodded my head and tried not to look smug. "Thank you, sir."

Mr. Albertson and I turned to leave.

"Miss Hunter?"

I paused on the threshold. "Yes, sir?"

"Remember you have until Monday. Understood?"

"Completely, sir." I hurried after Mr. Albertson.

Mr. Albertson walked even faster back to the classroom than he had going to the office, but I managed to keep up with him. Ignoring the students' stares, I followed him to his desk. Sylvia stood at the blackboard, watching each student with a hawk eye.

Mr. Albertson gestured to her. "Miss Sylvia, you may be seated."

Sylvia handed the piece of chalk back to Mr. Albertson and brushed past me on the way to her desk, giving me a tight smile.

I remained at the front of the room, afraid if I sat down that he would not give me the book.

Mr. Albertson settled behind his desk and opened a deep drawer. He fished out a book and slid it across to me without looking in my direction.

I picked up the book and headed back to my seat. Mr. Albertson propped his elbows on his desk and allowed his forehead to touch his hands.

None of the students moved. I wondered for a moment if he was praying. Then he raised his head.

"Turn to page 104 and 105. Do all of the problems."

Several students groaned. Mr. Albertson ignored them and simply stared into space until the end of the class period.

I struggled with the work, flipping back pages to find any information to help me. When he took up our work at the end of class, I had only managed to do five problems. And they were probably wrong.

Clothed In Thunder

Before we were allowed to leave, he pointed to the blackboard.

"Your homework for tomorrow. I expect everyone to have it. No excuses." He turned to me with narrowed eyes.

"Class dismissed."

Chapter 10--Michael & Dan

After school, I again went to Marla's and told her all about Michael's visit before we settled down to work. For the next three days after school, Marla patiently taught me lesson after lesson. I didn't know how I would ever pay her back.

The thought of seeing Michael kept me going through the rest of the week. With the exhaustion from trying to catch up on my math work, Mr. Albertson's daily disapproval, all my other homework, and the excitement of seeing Michael, I had all but forgotten Dan.

Dan showed up on Friday before Michael arrived. I had skipped going to Marla's, eager to get home from school. I had barely tossed my books on my bed when I heard the car drive into the yard. I ran out, hoping it was Michael, but already knowing it didn't sound like his truck.

Dan slammed his car door and grinned at me, his eyes sparkling in the afternoon sun.

I frowned at him, chided myself, and forced a smile. "Hey, Dan."

"Hey." He grinned at me. "I brought you something."

"What?" I didn't feel like playing guessing games with him.

I walked toward his car, and he held up a hand to stop me. "Wait right there."

I hesitated, irritated at his bossy tone. He swung open the car's back door, and a dog jumped out.

Chance!

I fell to my knees, and Chance bounded to me. His whole body wagged in excitement. My cries of happiness mingled with Chance's yelps. The other dogs ran around us, their barks adding to the commotion.

After a few minutes, Dan helped me to my feet. I placed a hand on his arm and looked up at him, unable to speak but grinning from ear to ear.

"Hey, Jay," a voice said behind me.

I spun around. "Michael! The dogs were making so much commotion we didn't hear you."

"Obviously," he said.

I started toward him, but the scowl on his face made me pause.

He raked his fingers through his hair. "Where do you want them?" he asked in a gruff voice.

"What?" I rubbed the palms of my hand on my dress, dismayed at his tone.

He jerked a thumb toward his truck with a horse trailer attached.

"Oh, you brought the horses. I'll go find Uncle Howard." I ran into the house, Chance on my heels.

Aunt Liza was in the kitchen preparing supper. "Did I hear your young men arriving?"

Heat rose to my cheeks. "Yes, Michael and Dan are outside. They have the horses, and they need Uncle Howard."

"He's gone to the store, and Zeke went with him. He'll be back in a few minutes. Go ahead and show them the barn. Your uncle already has the stalls ready."

I started back out and noticed Chance wagging his tail. "Aunt Liza? Dan brought Chance. I hope that was okay."

"Sure, hon. We told him he could," she said.

"Thank you." But my happiness in seeing Chance had been marred. Chance nudged my hand, and I absentmindedly patted his head then retraced my steps outside.

Michael and Dan both had their hands thrust in their pockets and were not speaking. Neither one looked at me.

"Uncle Howard's not here. The barn's down the road a piece."

Michael gave me a brief nod and walked to his truck.

I didn't wait for an invitation but climbed in on the passenger's side. I grabbed the door to close it, but Dan stopped me.

"I'll just ride with y'all," he said.

I looked nervously at Michael. He didn't speak, just tightened his grip on the steering wheel. I slid toward him, and Dan climbed in.

Michael cranked the trunk, and I pointed out the ruts that snaked through the trees. "Just follow the road."

He grunted. I was reminded of riding between Dan and Sylvia just the other day. But this was even worse.

Dan made small talk about folks back home. Neither Michael nor I spoke until the horses were being unloaded.

Dan led out a beautiful chestnut, and I caught my breath in surprise. "I thought you were bringing Blaze."

He shook his head. "Sold him and bought these two."

Michael held the halter of the other horse, an Appaloosa, white with gray spots. I frowned, puzzled. Why had Dan purchased two new horses? That didn't make sense when he was in the army. Was it just an excuse to visit me? Was that why Michael was so angry? I had to let Michael know that none of this was my doing.

Chance had followed us and sniffed the horses. Neither took any notice of him, but I called him away in case one took a notion to kick.

I followed Michael and Dan into the dark barn. "If you don't need my help. . ."

Dan shook his head. "Mike and I can handle it."

"Well, I'll just get back to the house and help Aunt Liza with supper. It'll be ready soon."

"Great!" Dan went into the stall to remove the chestnut's halter.

Michael followed me out. "I can't stay."

"Michael! I thought you were going to spend the weekend."

He shifted from one foot to another and stared over my shoulder, not meeting my eyes. "Sorry. Some things came up."

"Please?"

He cast a glance at me. "Maybe just for supper, then I've got to get back."

Was it because he was mad at me? Or, had Dan said something to anger him? Was he mad about the horses? Or, simply because I had thanked Dan for bringing Chance?

Clothed In Thunder

I didn't know what else to say, and his face looked so thunderous I was afraid I would say the wrong thing. I simply nodded and left.

As I neared the house, the smells drifting from the kitchen made my mouth water. I arrived just as Uncle Howard and Zeke got back from the store. They headed out to the barn, Zeke eager to see the horses. I set the table as Aunt Liza finished up the last of the cooking. Her scent of vanilla trailed behind her as she scurried around the kitchen.

When everyone arrived back, I helped her carry the food to the table. Zeke laughed at something Dan said. Michael, looking sullen, didn't speak. We gathered around the table, and Uncle Howard said the blessing.

Michael didn't eat much, just moved his food around on the plate. His bloodshot eyes steadily avoided me. Occasionally, he rubbed his unshaven chin. He only spoke when answering a question from Aunt Liza or Uncle Howard.

Dan praised Aunt Liza's cooking and talked with Uncle Howard of hunting, inviting him to deer hunt on his father's land when we visited at Christmas. He also gave Zeke attention, promising he would take him riding if Uncle Howard and Aunt Liza approved.

After supper, he even offered to help with the dishes, but Aunt Liza waved all of us away, telling us to go visit.

Michael shook his head. "I'd best be leaving. Thank you for supper."

He went out, into the night, and I followed after him. Ignoring me, he headed to his truck and reached behind the seat. In the light spilling from the house, I could see him raise a bottle to his lips and take a drink.

"What are you doing?" I asked.

He turned to face me. "I could ask the same of you."

"What have I done?"

"I dunno. You tell me." He gave me a long, cold stare.

"Michael, I'm sorry if you think I've done something wrong. But I haven't. You're being ridiculous."

"Am I?" He gave me an angry look, then pulled me to him and kissed me, his unshaven face scratching mine.

I pushed him away. "You're drunk."

"No, not yet." He took another swig from the bottle.

"Michael, I don't want you here drinking like this. What would Uncle Howard and Aunt Liza think?"

He laughed harshly. "That's a good one."

"What do you mean?"

His eyes narrowed. "Maybe you need to ask them."

"Are you saying they drink? You're drunk as a skunk if you believe that." Anger boiled inside me.

He shrugged his shoulders. "Forget them. Listen to me, Jay--are you going to tell Drake to clear out?"

I slowly shook my head. "It's not my house. I'm not the one who decides who stays."

He clenched his teeth. "You're not, heh?" He laughed harshly. "You'd best be getting back in to your company." He swung onto the running board of the truck.

"He's not my company!" I struggled to calm myself before I spoke again. "Michael . . . you can't leave like this. You're not in any shape to drive."

"I'm not? Just watch me." He dropped onto the seat, slammed the door, and gunned the motor.

He sped away, the horse trailer careening behind him. I clenched my hands into fists, the nails digging into my palms. How dare he act like this. . .drinking, making accusations? Well, if that was the way he wanted it, who needed him?

I stomped back to the porch, anger throbbing, my head aching, my heart breaking.

Chapter 11--Dan's Help

Before going in, I sat down in the swing, gulping in the night air as if it were water.

I missed Poppa so much! He could have told me what to do. Chance lay his head on my knee, and I buried my face into his fur.

The door squeaked open, and I straightened and slowed my breathing.

Dan. Without speaking, he sat down beside me.

"Michael leave?"

"Yes." I averted my eyes.

"I'm sorry if I caused you trouble. . ."

I plastered a smile on my face. "No trouble. Michael just needed to get home."

We swung in silence for a few minutes, and I shivered. I had run after Michael without even grabbing a sweater. "I best be getting back inside." I stood, and Dan got up at the same time.

He blocked my way, and I waited for him to move.

"Jay, your aunt was telling me that you're behind in your math."

I gritted my teeth, trying not to be irritated with Aunt Liza. "Yes, a little. I've got someone helping me."

"Listen, I'd be glad to help."

I looked at him in surprise. "Help?"

He chuckled softly. "I know my grades were never the best in the world, but I've always been good in math. I can help you."

I shrugged my shoulders. "Sure." My teeth chattered. "I really need to get inside."

"Oh, sorry!" He pulled off his jacket and wrapped it around me before I could protest.

I thanked him, and he swung the door open for me.

"Your uncle fixed a cot out in his shop for me. I'll see you tomorrow."

I nodded and rushed into the house, calling a good night to my family as I headed for my room.

I grabbed Poppa's Bible off the dresser, and my mother's picture fluttered to the floor. I picked it up, and, without undressing, I climbed under the covers. I was so cold that I left Dan's jacket on. I studied my real mother's picture and wondered if she had ever had a boyfriend before Poppa. If she had lived, would she have told me things I needed to know? Like how to deal with Michael?

I sighed. I was sure she wouldn't have liked Michael coming here drinking. Poppa wouldn't have either.

But Poppa had always taught me to forgive, hadn't he? Yet, Michael had accused my aunt and uncle of drinking. Isn't that what he meant? Or, was he talking about someone else? Someone else in my family? I shook my head. Michael was drunk. He didn't know what he was saying.

I tucked my mother's picture back into the Bible and climbed out of bed to set it on the dresser. I pulled the string attached to the light, and the room was plunged into darkness.

I lay back down and tried to sort through my feelings. Michael was only behaving this way because he was jealous. Jealous of Dan, of all people. All I needed to do was make him understand there was no need to be jealous. I would write him a long letter tomorrow and make him understand somehow. Once he got over his jealousy, he wouldn't drink. *Would he?*

Surely his jealousy was the only reason he was drinking. I just had to convince him he had no reason to feel that way.

Michael and I were meant to be together. Of that I was sure. Feeling better, I shrugged off Dan's jacket, let it fall to the floor, and immediately fell asleep.

"It's easy," Dan said. He scratched pencil against paper for a minute. "See? Do you understand this part?"

I nodded my head. Surprisingly, Dan was a good teacher, and I suddenly grasped concepts I had been struggling with.

"You do the next one." He pushed the paper to me.

I scribbled furiously. "Wow, that is easy."

He beamed at me, and I smiled back, relieved I was finally catching on.

Aunt Liza and Uncle Howard came into the kitchen.

Uncle Howard poured a cup of coffee from the pot on the back of the stove. "Y'all have been working all day. You need to take a break."

"Yes, sir," I said. "We were just finishing up."

"Time I got supper started," Aunt Liza said.

Dan stood and stretched. "I think I'll go riding. Would you like to go, Jay?"

There was nothing I'd rather do right then, but I shook my head. "No, I've got other homework and some other things to do." *Like writing Michael.*

Aunt Liza gazed at me. "Jay, fresh air would do you good. Go on with Dan."

I gathered up my book and papers. "No, ma'am. I've really got a lot to do. I'm sorry."

Dan flashed a smile, and his dimples deepened. "That's okay. Maybe Zeke would like to go?"

My heart leaped in my throat. What if Zeke fell off the horse? Maybe I should go to keep an eye on him.

I chided myself for my worry, knowing I couldn't always be with him.

I nodded my head. "I'm sure he'd love to go if Aunt Liza and Uncle Howard think it's okay."

"Just keep a close eye on him, Dan," Aunt Liza said. She went to the door and opened it to call Zeke.

I headed for my room. It was true I did have other homework, but it could wait. I pulled a clean sheet of paper out of my notebook and thought of what I wanted to say. After several attempts, I finally had what I thought was a good letter.

I reread it to make sure it was pleasant and cheerful but made sure I got my point across. I did not like Dan and never would. I didn't mention Michael's drinking or his accusations. There'd be time later to tackle that.

I folded the paper, slid it into an envelope, and addressed it. I went in search of a stamp, but Aunt Liza didn't have any. I would have to stop by the post office on the way home from school on Monday and buy one.

I finished my homework and Dan and Zeke came back, Zeke flushed, not just with the chilly fall air, but also the excitement of riding the horse.

Aunt Liza had finished supper, and we sat down to eat. Dan glanced at Zeke and me before he cleared his throat.

"Zeke and I've been talking. . ." He paused and glanced around the table. "A picture show just came out. . ."

"Can we go, Jay? Please?" Zeke said.

"Which one?" Aunt Liza asked before I could.

Dan smiled at Zeke who squirmed in his seat with excitement. "*Heidi.* It's about a young girl..."

"Who goes to live with her grandfather," I said. "I read the book."

Aunt Liza clapped her hands together. "I did, too. It was a wonderful book."

Zeke turned his pleading eyes on me. "Please?"

I shook my head at him. "We don't have the money."

"Dan said he would pay, didn't you, Dan?" Zeke looked from Dan to me.

Dan nodded. "Of course. My treat. I would like to take all of you." He glanced around the table.

Uncle Howard shook his head. "Sorry, son. I'm teaching Sunday School tomorrow. I need to prepare my lesson."

"Y'all go ahead and have a good time," Aunt Liza said. "I'll stay here and keep Howard company."

I was trapped. Zeke would never forgive me if we didn't go, and I couldn't let him go alone with Dan. And, I had to admit, it would be fun to go to a picture show.

I made up my mind and nodded my head. "All right. Let's get the kitchen cleaned, so we can get ready."

Zeke jumped from his seat and gave me a hug before carrying his dishes to the sink. I carried scraps out to feed Chance and the other dogs.

Michael could have been going with us if it had not been for his anger. On second thought, maybe he wouldn't. He never would have accepted Dan's charity, and I wasn't sure if he would want to spend his money.

I put thoughts of Michael aside, the best I could, and decided to enjoy myself. I went back inside to get ready.

Chapter 12--The Test

The show had been wonderful, and Zeke and I thanked Dan. He left on Sunday, right after services.

Monday, I tucked Michael's letter into my books, planning to buy a stamp after school. I felt confident, walking to school, knowing I was as prepared as I could be for the test Mr. Albertson planned for me. I put away my things and headed to my seat. Marla gave me an encouraging smile.

Mr. Albertson didn't waste any time. He had written a series of problems across the board and called me to the front as soon as class began. I stepped to the board with assurance.

When he handed me the chalk, I thought he'd put the other students to work. But, no, every eye watched me as I began, the chalk squeaking across the board.

My hands became sweaty, and I rubbed them, one at a time, on my dress. I could do this. Marla had helped me a lot, not to mention Dan. I had spent hours yesterday, on my own, pouring over the book.

I took a few deep breaths and concentrated on the problems, ignoring the stares from the class. I worked the first fairly simple problems quickly. Then I began to get bogged down. Each answer I wrote came after much mental toil.

I knew, though, that the answers were correct. If they hadn't been, I'm sure I would have heard snickers from the other students.

Instead, nothing but silence. Silence except for the ticking clock that hung above the blackboard and the chalk scratching across the board. Although cool in the room, sweat dripped from my brow. A trickle rolled down the side of my face, and I swiped it away.

Finally, I came to a problem that stumped me. I stepped back and looked at the five problems left. I furrowed my brow. No, I didn't remember any of it.

I shook my head, trying to clear it. No, I was sure neither Marla nor Dan had shown me problems like these. I handed the chalk back to Mr. Albertson.

"Why are you leaving problems unfinished?" he asked.

I met his gaze steadily, knowing I had done my best. "I don't know how to do them."

Feet shuffled. Marla had her hand in the air, waving frantically. Mr. Albertson ignored her. He walked to the board and studied my work. I heard a heavy sigh and glanced at Marla who still had her arm raised.

The slim boy with freckles, Andrew, I thought was his name, looked from me to her and shrugged. What was going on? Several people shook their heads, and two girls whose names I didn't know whispered together. Sylvia and her friends stared straight ahead.

Mr. Albertson marked two of my answers wrong plus the other five I had not attempted.

"Sixty-five per cent, Miss Hunter. Sixty-nine is a passing grade. Get your things. You'll be going back to ninth grade."

I grabbed my books from my desk before moving toward the cloakroom. Several students shuffled restlessly, and two other hands joined Marla's in the air.

Mr. Albertson ignored them.

"Class, open your book to page . . ."

"Mr. Albertson," Marla said firmly. She rose to her feet. "You gave Jay. . .Sarah Jane problems from chapters we have not covered yet."

Several voices assented. I stopped at the cloakroom door.

"Miss Phillips, when I want your opinion, I'll ask for it." He walked to where she stood and glared at her. "Sit down."

She obeyed reluctantly. I ducked into the cloakroom.

Marla had stood up for me. And others, too. Waves of emotion washed over me. My heart swelled in my chest, and I blindly gathered my sweater and syrup can.

Several students still mumbled under their breath when I slipped out the door.

I now knew the way to the office and found it easily. Miss Ballard raised her eyebrows at me when I arrived at the counter.

"I wondered if I could resell these books to you. I'll need ninth grade books."

She moved from behind her desk and placed her hand on mine. "Oh, sweetie. You didn't pass your exam?"

I shook my head. "No, ma'am. Mr. Albertson said I didn't."

Mr. Martin came out of his office. "Miss Ballard, I need you to . . ."

Miss Ballard interrupted him. "Miss Hunter didn't pass her exam."

I met his eyes without flinching.

"Miss Hunter, I believe you told me you were going to work hard and catch up with the other students." He surveyed me solemnly.

"I did my best, Mr. Martin."

He rubbed his chin. "That's all anyone can ever ask." He turned toward his office and paused. "Miss Ballard, I need to see you when you finish here."

"Yes, sir." She turned back to me. "Let's see if we can trade these books in."

She made friendly conversation as she searched for the books. "Are you settling in okay at your aunt and uncle's?

"Yes, ma'am."

"That's good. Remember what I told you? If you ever need anything, just let me know."

"Yes, ma'am. I will. Thank you."

I took the books she offered and walked out of the office. The bell rang, and the students milled out into the hallway. Someone caught me by the arm. It was Marla.

"He's not going to get away with this." She ground her teeth.

The vehemence in her voice surprised me. "Marla! I don't want you to get in trouble."

"Don't worry about that. My daddy is a member of the school board. And he's also the best man in the world." She jutted out her chin.

I couldn't suppress a smile as I patted the hand that still held my arm. "Really, it's okay. I'll be fine."

"I know you will. But I won't. I've got to get to class. See you later." She scurried away.

I found my next class on the schedule and noticed one good thing. Miss Weaver was going to be my homeroom teacher. Thank God for the small things. And the big things too. Ninth grade wouldn't be so bad. And I had Michael's letter all ready to mail. When he read it, I was sure he would understand, and things would be back to normal.

After school, I walked to the post office, feeling good, discovering I had friends who supported me, and now about to mail the letter that would make everything right with Michael.

I was at the counter, buying a stamp, when Sylvia and her chorus of friends tramped in.

She placed her hand on my arm, as if we were old friends.

"That Michael is a fun guy," she said. Her friends giggled.

I wrinkled my forehead. "Michael?"

"Yes. Michael Hutchinson."

"Michael Hutchinson?" Surely, she didn't mean Michael. I looked down at the letter in my hand, and her gaze followed mine.

"Oh, you're mailing him a letter?"

Curiosity got the best of me. "What do you mean, a 'fun guy'?"

"Some friends were having a party Friday night. You could say he crashed the party." She giggled along with her friends.

"Crashed?"

"Yes, he drove his truck into the gate."

Fear clutched my heart. "What? Was he hurt?"

"No, he was fine. More than fine I'd say." She raised one eyebrow and grinned. "Pop wasn't too happy when Michael brought me home after midnight on Friday."

It was as if Sylvia were speaking a foreign language. I stared at her dumbly.

"Pop almost didn't let me go out with him Saturday night." She poked out her bottom lip in a juvenile expression. "I had to beg and plead before he gave in."

"Saturday night? Michael was here on Saturday?"

"Yes. . ." She stepped back and feigned surprise. "He's not a boyfriend, is he?" She smirked and tapped me on the arm playfully. "Now, Sarah Jane, you've got that good-looking Dan Drake. You can't keep all the best-looking guys for yourself." This sent her friends off into new peals of laughter.

"Dan Drake is not my boyfriend," I spat out.

Sylvia arched her brows. "Well, Michael thinks he is. Especially after he saw you going to the picture show with him."

"Michael saw me?" My face burned, and I swallowed the lump in my throat.

She nodded her head, and I turned away, unable to speak, unable to bear more.

Clothed In Thunder

I made it out to the sidewalk, the letter still clutched in my hand. I stared at it, then stumbled home and went into the kitchen. Aunt Liza was not there, and I was glad.

I opened the door on the wood-burning stove and thrust the letter in. I watched it burn before going to my room and weeping bitterly, the pain almost more than I could bear.

Chapter 13--Trip to the Office

The next day, I walked to school alone for the first two blocks, not even noticing anything around me. Sadness dogged my steps.

It wasn't until someone spoke that I saw two others had fallen in step beside me. I recognized them from the tenth-grade class. The boy was the one who had given the report in Miss Weaver's class. I didn't know the girl's name. They looked similar with freckles sprinkled across their noses and with green eyes.

"Hi, Sarah Jane," the boy said. He ran a hand through his brown hair, pushing it away from his face.

"Hi. . .Andrew?"

"Right, I'm Andrew, and this is my sister Anne."

His sister smiled at me, showing dimples. "We're twins, in case you were wondering. People call us Raggedy Ann and Andy." She made a face.

"Raggedy Ann and Andy?"

"You've never heard of the dolls?" Andrew asked.

I shook my head.

Anne grinned from ear to ear. "Maybe she won't be making fun of us!"

"I've never seen the dolls," I said.

"Red yarn for hair, button eyes?"

I shook my head again. "Doesn't ring a bell."

"You must really be from the boondocks," Andrew said.

"Andrew, that's rude!" Anne punched her brother's arm.

Andrew looked sheepish. "I'm sorry. I didn't mean to offend you."

"That's okay. I probably am from the boondocks."

"Boondocks or not, Mr. Albertson had no right to treat you the way he did," Andrew said.

Anne shook her head, sending the short, brown curls bouncing. "Right. You did great on the math problems. He gave you the hardest ones."

"And Marla was right. Those last problems came from chapters we haven't covered yet," Andrew said.

I shrugged my shoulders. "It's okay. It's too late to do anything about it now."

Andrew laughed. "Oh, no it's not. Marla will take care of this." His eyes sparkled.

"Yeah, Marla will take care of it or die trying," his sister agreed.

I looked at them and frowned. Would Marla really do something? If she did, Mr. Albertson would get angry at her, and I didn't want her to get into trouble. I shook my head slowly. "I hope she doesn't."

"Just you wait and see. Once Marla gets hold of something, she's like a snapping turtle. She won't let it go 'til lightning strikes." Andrew grinned.

Mild-mannered Marla? Marla with the soft voice? But she did sound vehement yesterday. . .

Hope fluttered in me as we approached the stone steps. Maybe I could go back to tenth grade. I started to smile but frowned instead.

Sylvia and her friends waited at the bottom of the steps, and my face burned. They smiled as we approached. I figured they were smiling at Anne and Andrew, but the twins continued without even glancing in her direction. I, too, tried to walk by, but Sylvia called my name.

"Good morning," she said, the smile growing broader.

A chorus of good mornings came from her friends.

I stared at them, puzzled.

Sylvia danced over to where I stood and linked her arm through mine. "We'll walk with you."

"Uh, sure." I wanted to shake her off, but then she would know how she had hurt me yesterday.

"Michael's so handsome," she whispered in my ear, repeating what she had said yesterday. She squeezed my arm. "Is he your boyfriend?"

I hesitated. Was he anymore? Drinking, going out with Sylvia? I sadly shook my head. "No, guess not."

She released my arm. "See you later." She walked away, and her friends gathered around her, whispering and giggling.

I stared after them. Had I just given her permission to date Michael? I shrugged my shoulders. What did it matter, anyway? She'd already dated him.

But. . .what if she was lying? Maybe it hadn't happened like she said. Maybe I needed to see Michael and get his side of it.

As I neared my new homeroom, Miss Weaver's class, I spied Marla waiting by the door. A man stood next to her. I knew immediately it was her father although he had never been at home when I visited. She looked remarkably like him, except he did not have her buck teeth. He flashed a smile at me, and I immediately fell under his spell.

"I'm Jackson Phillips. I've heard so much about you, Jay. Marla's told me what's happened here."

I blushed. "That's okay. Really, I don't want to make a fuss."

"Nonsense. We'll have this cleared up in no time. Principal Martin and Mr. Albertson are waiting for us in the office."

My stomach did flip flops. "I need to tell Miss Weaver."

"No need. I've already spoken to her. Ladies?" He held out his arms, one to Marla and one to me.

I had no choice. I took his arm. Marla tilted her chin up in an imitation of her father. I drew a trembling breath, and we headed down the hall. Students parted before us.

We arrived at the office, and Mr. Phillips held the door for us. Marla waited for me to go first.

Miss Ballard stood at the ready, obviously expecting us. She smiled at Mr. Phillips, and I realized he was held in great esteem by everyone. We entered Principal Martin's office. Both the principal and Mr. Albertson were standing, waiting for us.

They shook hands with Mr. Phillips. Principal Martin pulled two chairs forward for Marla and me. I thanked him and sat down.

When everyone had been seated, Mr. Phillips spoke.

"Mr. Albertson, I believe a misunderstanding occurred yesterday." He rubbed his chin, smiling gently.

Mr. Albertson wrung his hands together. "Yes, sir. Inadvertently I tested Miss Hunter on math concepts beyond the level on which we are currently working. Removing those math problems from consideration, Miss Hunter did pass the test." His Adam's apple bobbed up and down as he waited for Mr. Phillips to speak.

Mr. Phillips nodded curtly at Mr. Albertson. He stood and addressed Principal Martin. "I take it everything is in order now for Miss Hunter to return to tenth grade?"

"Yes, of course. Miss Ballard will get her the necessary books." He looked in my direction. "I'm sorry for any inconvenience this may have caused you, Miss Hunter."

"Yes, Miss Hunter. Entirely my fault," Mr. Albertson said. A bead of sweat lay above his upper lip, and he wiped it away.

I rose, my legs shaky. I murmured something in reply, and Marla and I left. Mr. Phillips stayed behind with Mr. Albertson and Principal Martin.

I gave Marla a hug. "Thank you," I whispered.

"My pleasure. I'll see you in class." She walked away with a confident step.

I could believe it was her pleasure from the look on her face.

Miss Ballard already had the tenth-grade books waiting for me. She told me I could return the ninth-grade books later.

Again, she reminded me to let her know if I ever needed anything. Did she tell all students this, or was it because I was friends with Mr. Phillips' daughter?

I thanked her and promised I would. I tucked the books under my arm and left. I noticed that these, while not new, were not the tattered ones I had before. I smiled at Miss Ballard's kindness.

When I walked in the classroom, the class burst into applause, even Sylvia and her friends. I ducked my head, my cheeks burning, and found my seat.

The class whispered for a minute before Sylvia shushed them. Order was restored and heads bent over books, pencils scratching on paper when Mr. Albertson returned. He didn't speak, simply took the chalk from Sylvia and wrote problems on the board. Then he sat down behind his desk, lacing his fingers together.

At least, I could work hard to prove Marla's faith in me.

I had to just keep swimming.

Or at least not sink.

Chapter 14--Thunder & Lightning

We received letters from Dan, thanking Uncle Howard and Aunt Liza for boarding his horses. His tone was friendly. Maybe he really had changed. I didn't hear from Michael but hadn't expected to, had I?

I wrote to Dan and thanked him for helping with my math work.

I started exercising the horses every chance I could. Zeke often came with me, riding the Appaloosa who was less spirited than the chestnut. Dan had not told us their names, and Zeke urged me to write him to find out.

Dan responded that he hadn't named them and for us to decide. His letter was addressed to both Zeke and me, and that made me feel better. One strange thing was that he had signed it "Daniel." Somehow, this seemed to fit him now.

Clothed In Thunder

Zeke and I walked to the pasture early one Saturday. We leaned against the fence and watched the horses prancing, energized by a cold front that had moved in.

"Thought of any names yet?" I asked Zeke.

He rubbed his nose that was red from the cool air. "Did you hear what the preacher read last Sunday?"

I wasn't sure what he meant. "What part?"

"The part about horses."

I scrunched my forehead and tried to remember the sermon. "His sermon was about Job, wasn't it?"

"Yeah, do you remember?"

I shook my head, ashamed Zeke remembered, and I didn't. "Sorry."

"Something about clothes," Zeke said.

"Clothes?" My brow cleared. "Oh, I know what you're talking about. "*Hast thou clothed his neck in thunder?*"

"Yeah, that was it. That was about horses. We can name one Thunder, can't we? And the other one Lightning?"

I laughed. "Reckon so. Which one will be Thunder?"

He furrowed his brow and studied the horses. "The red one will be Red Thunder and the other one White Lightning."

My knuckles turned white as I gripped the post. But Zeke didn't know white lightning referred to moonshine. He didn't know about drunkenness. *About Michael.*

I looked at him sadly. Let's just go with Whitey for the white one. Red and Whitey. Okay?"

He shrugged. "Okay. Are we going to ride today?"

"Sure."

He scampered ahead of me, blissfully unaware, and I wanted to protect him, to save him from pain, but knew that was all part of living.

But happiness was all part of living, too. I followed after Zeke, putting Michael out of my mind, determined to enjoy our ride, to grab what happiness I could.

That night, I wrote Dan and told him the names, Red and Whitey. Not very original but good enough.

I groomed the horses every day. I would have ridden more if not for school work and chores I had to do. Uncle Howard rode the horses since he had plenty of time. He was unable to find much work for his woodworking shop.

The days continued getting shorter. Thanksgiving came, and Aunt Liza cooked a delicious meal of roasted chicken, dumplings, sweet potatoes, and the best pecan pie I had ever tasted. Time seemed to speed up between

Thanksgiving and the day school was to let out for the Christmas holidays.

Report cards were handed out that day. Mr. Albertson gave out the report cards in homeroom with our math grades recorded, yet, he made it a point to call me to his desk.

"Miss Hunter, normally I would give a student an A- for a 93 average, even though we're on a seven-point scale and that is technically, a B+. With your. . ." He cleared his throat. ". . .attitude, however, I know you are not an A student, and, therefore, I gave you what you made. I hope you understand."

"Yes, sir. I understand." I guessed that he was telling me so I wouldn't report to Marla's father. And I promised myself I wouldn't complain, although I returned to my desk seething. Just because I didn't have the math background when I first arrived did not mean I was not an A student. To go from where I started, knowing nothing, up to a 93 was something he should have commended me for.

I vowed I'd show him before the year was out that I *was* an A student.

One thing I was grateful for. Mr. Albertson did not take his anger out on Marla. If anything, he treated her with more deference.

In my other classes I received A's. Miss Weaver had written a comment on my report card: *Excellent student!*

Clothed In Thunder

I hugged Marla good-bye after school. Uncle Howard and Aunt Liza were taking Zeke and me home for the Christmas holidays.

I both dreaded and looked forward to going. I really wanted to see Aunt Jenny, Uncle Colt, Laurie, and William. But we also planned to go by to see Momma at the mental hospital. I wasn't sure how she would react when she saw us.

And then there was Michael. Would I see him when I was there? Would he come over? I held out little hope. Besides, did I want to if he was still drinking? But maybe he had quit. Maybe it was just because he was upset that day.

And, maybe, Sylvia had lied to me. I needed to talk to Michael, to get his side of the story, to find out if Sylvia had made up going out with him just to upset me.

Uncle Howard had borrowed a truck, and we all squeezed together in the cab. Aunt Liza sat in the middle and Zeke in my lap. I stared out the window, not really seeing the barren trees we drove by.

Sylvia had not mentioned Michael again. If he had been back to Plainsville, I didn't know of it. All of this between us had been a misunderstanding--that was all.

By the time we arrived, I had convinced myself Michael and I could work things out. I actually was looking forward to seeing him and planned to seek him out if he didn't come over.

But I didn't have to. It was the day after we got there, on Christmas Day, when he showed up.

We were still eating pecan pie and egg custard when William answered the door. Michael seemed almost like someone I didn't know. Still, I was happier than I had been in ages just to see his face.

He sat on the hearth, and Aunt Jenny brought him a slice of pie and a glass of milk. I stayed with the women in the kitchen, putting things away while the men gathered around the fireplace, swapping stories about hunting or fishing.

I peered out the door. Michael talked, but his laughter seemed forced, and his face was strained and white.

I was drying the dishes when he appeared at my side.

"Jay, I need to speak to you." He didn't wait for me to answer but simply strode away.

I hastily dried my hands and pulled off the apron and hurried after him. He had walked outside and stood under the naked branches of the large pecan tree that stood near the back corner of the house. My heart thundered in my chest.

His dark hair shone in the weak rays of the winter sun, and he raked his fingers through it and spoke without looking at me. "Why did you accept Drake's horses as a gift?"

Chapter 15--The Fight

Of anything I expected him to say, this wasn't it. "What?"

"Why did you accept the horses as a gift?" he repeated, his voice calm, although he still did not look at me.

"They weren't a gift for me." My voice trembled with nervousness. Hadn't I wondered about the horses myself? But I didn't know Daniel bought them for *me*, did I?

"Do you deny you have been taking care of them?" His voice remained calm.

"Uncle Howard is boarding his horses. Daniel asked me to exercise them. That's all there is to it."

"Daniel? When have you ever called him Daniel?" He turned to glare at me.

I knew I had said the wrong thing and took a step back. I shrugged my shoulders. "I guess that's the name he's using now."

"And how would you know?"

I kept silent, knowing if I told him that Daniel. . .Dan and I had been writing, he would be furious. But it wasn't like that. Zeke and I wrote him together, and he always included both of us when he wrote back.

"You could have told him to find someplace else to board the horses." The anger drained from his voice. "Why didn't you say no?"

I sighed. "Michael, it wasn't my decision. Why don't you believe me?"

He stared at me for a second as if he didn't know me. "Dan's in love with you. Everyone knows it. And you keep encouraging him."

"Encouraging? What do you mean?"

"I saw the look on your face. How happy you were when we brought the horses."

"He brought me Chance. I was just thanking him." Anger boiled up. "Let me ask you a question. Why didn't you bring me Chance? Why did you let Daniel. . .Dan bring him?"

He raked the fingers through his hair again. "Because it was his idea." He narrowed his eyes. "He has better ideas. Is that what you want me to say? He's richer, and drives a fancy car, and can give you an expensive horse. . ."

"And he doesn't go out with girls named Sylvia." I spat it out before I could help myself.

Michael gave me a long hard look. "I did not go out with her. Who told you that?"

"She did," I said quietly.

His eyebrows drew together, and he shook his head as if trying to rid it of cobwebs. "I don't remember it."

"Did you stay the weekend you brought the horses? Were you there on Saturday?"

"Yeah."

"Why can't you remember if you went out with Sylvia?" My heart thundered in my chest. *Why was he lying to me?* "What *do* you remember? Did you see me go to the picture show with Daniel?"

His head jerked up. "What?"

This was not going the way I had planned. I reached out to stroke Michael's arm, catching the scent of his cologne. Only now I knew he used it to cover the smell of alcohol. I stepped away from him.

He jammed his hands in his pockets. "You went out with him?" he asked quietly.

"No! He took Zeke, and I went along."

He narrowed his eyes. "Just because Zeke was along doesn't make it better."

"Michael, you either trust me or you don't. I'm through apologizing for. . . for no reason."

"I'll trust you if you never write or speak to Drake again."

"And this coming from you? Going out with Sylvia behind my back? How dare you say that when you've been doing things a lot worse than me?"

"I told you I wasn't with Sylvia." He stared down at the ground. "At least, I can't remember."

"How can you not remember? Were you that drunk?"

"If you want the truth, yes, I was *that* drunk. I drank until I passed out in my truck. Happy?"

I took a step toward him and hit him in the chest with the heel of my hand. "Why? Why are you drinking?"

He caught my wrist and shoved me away. "Always have. Always will, I reckon." His look of defiance pierced my heart.

"Always? What do you mean?"

He raked back his hair again. "Drake and I started drinking when we were around eleven or so." He shrugged his shoulders. "It's no big deal."

"No big deal? You can't even remember that weekend!"

"What did you expect? When I saw you smiling up at Drake. . ."

"So, is this what you're going to do whenever you get upset? Drink yourself into oblivion?" My hands shook, and I clasped them together.

"Beats the alternative."

I stamped my feet in frustration.

He eyed me for a few seconds, his face hard. "Promise me you will not speak to Drake again."

"I'll speak to whomever I want to, Michael Hutchinson. You will not tell me how to pick my friends. Do you understand?"

He raked his hair back with both hands. "Fine. If you prefer Drake over me, that's your choice." He glared at me. "But neither will you pick *my* friends." He strode away but stopped midway to his truck. "*And you're sure not going to tell me when I can drink*. Especially since. . ." He threw his hands up in a gesture of frustration.

"Especially what?"

He kept going without answering. I gritted my teeth to keep from screaming at him.

He climbed in his truck and drove away. Let him go. I didn't need his jealous fits. Or, his drinking.

Why had I never known it? How did he hide it all this time? But really, how often had I been around him for very long? Three or four times? Tears slid down my face. I really had not known him at all.

I looked toward the house. I didn't want to go inside. Instead, I walked to Cedar Spring, blinded by my tears. It wasn't until I climbed the path that the tears began to abate. I entered the clearing, and the peaceful surroundings calmed me.

The sun still shone, surprising me. It felt as if I had argued with Michael all day. It probably wasn't later than one or two o'clock. I sat down with my back to the tree. Emerald sunlight filtered through the branches.

Things were supposed to be better. Wasn't that the promise of the cedar? Maybe God had other plans for me, other lessons for me to learn.

Was I wrong? Michael and I weren't meant to be together? The cold realization that I may never see him again washed over me.

My heart felt as if it were breaking in two. I laid my head on my knees and sobbed. For the loss of Michael, for the loss of Poppa, even for the loss of Momma, and for the mother I had never known.

Maybe Michael had always just felt sorry for me, never really cared for me at all. Why? Why had Michael done this to me?

My sobbing increased in volume, and I felt a hand on my shoulder.

I looked up into Laurie's face. She dropped to her knees by my side. "Jay, what's wrong?"

I couldn't answer. I fell against her, my head lying across her legs. She pushed the hair away from my face and made shushing noises. It only made me cry more.

"Jay, please. You're scaring me. What's wrong?"

I struggled to sit up, to control my crying.

Laurie wrapped an arm around me. "Are you hurt?" she asked gently.

I didn't answer, just laid my head on her shoulder and sobbed.

"You and Michael have a fight?"

I nodded miserably. Laurie pushed me gently back until I leaned against the cedar.

"Wait here. I'll go wet my handkerchief in the steam."

I gulped a few unsteady breaths and tried to staunch the flow of tears. She returned with the handkerchief, and I took it from her and wiped my face. It was icy cold from the stream. I had gone out without a coat and only now noticed the cold breeze. I shivered.

"We need to get inside, out of the cold," Laurie said.

"I don't want anyone to see me." I twisted the handkerchief.

"Everyone was in the front room when I left. We'll go in the back door and you can go in my room."

"Okay." I stood up on legs that wobbled.

Laurie wrapped her arm around my waist, and I allowed her to lead me away from the cedar, away from the clearing, and out onto the road.

I felt ashamed for crying so much. I struggled to contain my tears, especially as we neared the house. Laurie checked, and the back room was still empty. I scooted to her room and lay down on her bed. She followed in a little while with a wet wash cloth.

"I told them you weren't feeling well."

"That's the truth," I said with a feeble smile.

Laurie wiped my forehead with the cool cloth, and I let her, feeling too weak to protest.

"Do you want to talk about what happened?" She gazed at me solemnly.

I closed my eyes. "Nothing, really. Michael's jealous of Daniel."

"Daniel?"

"Drake."

Laurie snorted. "Jealous of Drake? That's ridiculous."

"I know. I've tried to tell him I only went to see *Heidi* because of Zeke."

"You went with Drake to the picture show? Are you as crazy as a June bug on a string?"

I opened my eyes. She was staring at me as if she had never seen me before. Her face softened as she continued looking at me. "Jay, I'm sorry. I'm just surprised."

I nodded my head. "It's okay. I didn't want to have anything to do with Daniel to begin with. But he really has changed."

Laurie snorted again and was immediately apologetic. "I shouldn't have done that." She looked down at her hands contritely. "It's just hard to imagine him changing."

I sat up and leaned against the wall. "He's really been nice. He helped me with my math work."

Laurie's eyes widened, and she shook her head at me. "I see now why Michael's so mad."

"But I don't like Daniel! You know I don't. I'm just trying to do the right thing." I reached over and touched her arm. "I'm trying to do the Christian thing and treat Daniel right. And Michael should trust me."

"You've taken a liking to Drake. Leastwise, that's the way it sounds to me."

"Laurie!" Fresh tears sprang to my eyes.

She pulled me into a hug. "Please don't cry."

She gave me the wash rag, and I swiped at my eyes. I fumbled for my handkerchief and blew my nose. "Probably it's all for the best. I've got to finish high school. Michael wants to go to college." I didn't want to tell her about his drinking, feeling ashamed.

"He's going to API next semester," she said.

My heart beat a little faster. "Really?" I thought he wouldn't begin until the fall."

"No. He had enough credits to graduate early."

I slumped back down on the bed. "It doesn't matter. He doesn't want to see me ever again." *And I didn't want to see him. Not as long as he drank.*

Laurie grabbed my arm and pulled me to my feet. "Come on and fix your hair. You've moped around enough. There's still plenty of pie left."

"I guess you're right. If I stay here, I'll probably just start crying again." I let out a long, shuddering breath and did as Laurie asked.

Chapter 16--Visit to Momma

The next morning all I wanted to do was go home to Plainsville, but Aunt Jenny and Uncle Colt had planned to take us to see Momma.

Aunt Jenny and Aunt Liza were cooking breakfast when I woke up. I dragged myself into the kitchen, my eyes feeling swollen and grainy. Aunt Jenny refused the offer of my help.

I sat down at the table, and she brought me a cup of coffee although I usually didn't drink it. The house was quiet except for the sounds of frying bacon and sausage. My aunts kept stealing covert stares at me.

"Where is everyone?" I asked.

"They're all gone out to the barn to do the chores," Aunt Jenny said.

"Zeke, too?"

"Yes. He's been up since the crack of dawn. He's excited about going to see your momma today." Aunt Liza rolled out biscuits and patted them into the iron skillet.

I sighed. *Momma.* Just one more thing I would have to deal with. "How is Momma, Aunt Jenny?"

"I think she's some better. Still depressed, but the doctors are still adjusting her medicines." She wiped her hands on her apron and came over to me. "Have you told Zeke that she's not your mother?"

I shook my head.

Aunt Liza slid the pan of biscuits into the oven and turned to face me. "Jenny and I have been talking. We think someone needs to talk to him before you go to see her. She might say something."

"Do you want me to talk to him?" Aunt Jenny asked, her eyes filled with concern.

I shook my head. "No. I need to." I chewed my bottom lip. I'd better do it now while the biscuits were baking. I pulled myself to my feet and went out to find him.

My hands were thrust deep into the pockets of my new coat. Well, it wasn't new. It was one of Aunt Liza's old ones. I thought of the gloves, scarves, and coats Momma had kept in her trunk. And that secret buried beneath them I had found. The secret that changed my life.

Tears sprang to my eyes, and I swiped at them.

All of that was in the past. I lived with my mother's sister now. And Aunt Liza was already becoming like the mother I had never had--a mother who loved me.

So what if I didn't have Michael? I still had people who loved me.

Zeke was in the barn with Laurie. The comforting smells of cows and pigs washed over me. I again had to blink back the tears.

What was wrong with me? Was I going to start crying all the time now?

Laurie threw me a look of concern. "Hey, Jay."

I smoothed my hair back. "I know I look terrible. . ."

"Like something the cat dragged in that the kittens wouldn't have?"

I remembered her saying that before. At a terrible time in my life. I shrugged. "Reckon I do."

"I reckon you have a right to. But you really don't look bad. Your eyes are a little red is all."

Zeke looked at me. "What's wrong, Jay?"

"Nothing to worry about." I held my hand out to Zeke. "I need to talk to you, though."

He placed his hand in mine, and we walked out of the warmth of the barn.

I led him to the front porch. We both sat down on the edge with our legs dangling over the side.

It was a moment before I spoke, remembering the night he had caught the lightning bugs. . .that night. . .

I pushed the thought firmly out of my mind. Poppa was gone, and there was no need dwelling on it. We had to get on with our own lives.

I draped my arm over his shoulders. "Zeke, I need to tell you something."

He beat his heels against the side of the porch. "What?"

"Momma's not my momma."

He frowned. "Momma's not your momma?"

"No, we have different mothers."

"You're not my sister?" Worry clouded his eyes.

"Yes, I'm your sister! We have the same father just different mothers." I squeezed him to me, and he laid his head against me for a few seconds before pulling away.

"Good. I'm glad you're my sister. Can I go back to the barn now?"

I smiled to myself. "It's about time for breakfast. Go see if you can round everyone up."

He jumped down and scurried off.

Well, that was easier than I thought. I climbed to my feet and went back in. At least I still had Zeke.

A stab of fear pierced my heart. I pushed away the thought that I might lose him, too. No need borrowing trouble from tomorrow, Poppa had always said.

After breakfast, we got ready to go see Momma. Aunt Liza and Uncle Howard with William and Laurie thought it best that they stayed home. We still didn't want Momma to know where Zeke and I had been living.

Aunt Jenny and Uncle Colt had visited Momma several times in the couple of months we had been gone.

On the way, Aunt Jenny cautioned us that Momma still struggled with depression. Zeke didn't know what that meant, and I explained that she was very sad. I knew the feeling.

I pretended, for Zeke's sake, to be happy. He clung to me when we arrived at the sanatorium. His grip tightened when we entered the common room. Several patients visited with their families. Momma sat at a small table next to the window, staring out.

She remained stiff and still as we approached. She didn't turn her vacant eyes on us until Aunt Jenny touched her shoulder.

"How are you, Molly?" Aunt Jenny asked.

Momma tried to smile. "I'm doing better."

"Hi, Momma," I said, kissing her forehead. Zeke hung back, but I pulled him forward. "Here's Zeke."

She held out her arms to him, and a lump came to my throat. Zeke climbed into her lap, and the rest of us gathered around the table. Momma took a long look at me.

"What's wrong with you, Sarah Jane? You been sick?"

"No, ma'am. I'm doing fine."

"We're so proud of her," Uncle Colt said. "She made five A's and a B+ on her report card."

Momma ignored Uncle Colt. Aunt Jenny cast him a glance, and they shared a look before Aunt Jenny turned back to Momma.

"Is there anything we can get you, Molly?"

"You can get me out of this place. Ain't nothing wrong with me." She stared in Aunt Jenny's eyes defiantly.

"Now, Molly. You know the doctor will release you as soon as you're better."

Momma laughed. "He just wants to keep me here for the money you're a paying him." Then she looked contrite. "Sorry. I'm just ready to get home. I think I'm better."

Uncle Colt rubbed his chin. "That's why you need to cooperate. You can get out a lot faster if you'll do what the doctor tells you."

Momma caught my eyes again. "I need to tell you what happened." Her eyes glazed over, and she began to speak. "One night, after we'd gone to sleep, the house caught on fire."

I started to interrupt, wondering why she was telling the story again, but Aunt Jenny put her finger to her lips.

"I heard someone yelling." Momma's voice cracked, and she took a deep breath before continuing. "I got up but didn't know where I was. The smoke had confused me. Someone grabbed me and pulled me through the window." She looked at me. "It was your father. He went in for my husband but came back without him." Her face contorted. "It was two o'clock in the morning. Your father was drunk. He always blamed his drunkenness for not being able to save my husband." She rubbed her temples.

"Poppa was drunk?" Zeke said.

"Drunk as a skunk," Momma said.

Aunt Jenny cleared her throat. "Remember, Molly, he had just lost his wife. He was grieving and wasn't himself."

Did all men drink? Because they just couldn't face reality? But Poppa had quit, hadn't he? He never drank. But what if he did, and I just didn't know? Could he have hidden it from me, just as Michael had? I shook my head, trying to understand, to remember Poppa. No, I was sure he didn't drink. Momma had continued with her story.

"I was in the hospital for a while. He came to visit me every single day. Brought me flowers."

Momma's eyes were on me as if waiting for me to speak.

I didn't know what she wanted me to say. "I don't know why you didn't tell me that you weren't my real mother," I finally said.

"I didn't see any reason. I decided to treat you like my own daughter. I did what I could. Not that you cared."

My fault for failing her? Just like her to place the blame on me. Her time here had not changed her at all. Instead of anger, though, her words only increased my sadness.

Uncle Colt tried to change the subject. "Did you ever want to move back to Birmingham?"

"Wanting to get rid of me?" She cocked one eyebrow at him.

"Of course not," Uncle Colt said, shaking his head slowly. "Molly, you know we'd do all we can to help you."

Momma clamped her lips together as if she didn't believe him.

"We need to get going." Aunt Jenny stood and gave Momma a hug. Momma continued sitting, her back stiff.

Uncle Colt simply patted her shoulder.

Momma kissed both Zeke's cheeks before letting him down. I started to lean over to kiss her, but she put a hand up to stop me.

Chapter 17--Clothed In Thunder

*M*omma's eyes clouded with pain. "No need pretending you care about me. Now that you know I'm not your real mother." She narrowed her eyes as if daring me to deny it.

"Momma," I said, keeping my voice as soft as I could. "You took care of me when I was little. I appreciate everything you did for me." I gave her a peck on the forehead and held out my hand to Zeke.

She nodded. "Zeke looks well. Thank you for taking care of him while I can't." She turned her head away.

Had she hidden her face so we wouldn't see her tears? What I said had been true. Maybe she did care for me in a way I couldn't understand. Maybe she *had* done her best.

Zeke and I followed our aunt and uncle outside. As we emerged into the sunlight, Zeke tilted his head up at me, his eyes hopeful. "She was better, wasn't she, Jay?"

"I hope so Zeke." I tousled his hair as we walked away from the mental hospital. He missed her. But that was only natural. She had always been nicer to him than she had been to me. At least up until Poppa died.

"Can we come back again, Jay?"

"Next time we visit. Maybe she'll be back home by then."

His face lit up. "I hope so."

My heart constricted. What if she did get out? Would Zeke choose her over me? My shoulders drooped. I didn't know what I'd do if I lost him, too.

But maybe that day would never come.

We stayed one more night before heading back to Plainsville. We stopped at the same gas station Michael had stopped at when we had first traveled to my aunt and uncle's. I refused the offer of a Coke, not wanting anything to remind me of Michael.

I was glad to be home, and I snuggled into the feather bed with three quilts on top of me. But I didn't sleep. I thought of Michael and how things had gone wrong so quickly. It seemed everything in life I loved, I lost.

Anger coursed through me. Why was God doing this to me?

Didn't I deserve some happiness?

I tossed and turned until the wee hours of the morning.

After my fitful night's sleep, I slipped out of the house before anyone else was up. Bundled against the chilly morning air, I slapped a saddle on Red to go for a quick ride.

Red was frisky from not being ridden for a couple of days. He broke into a gallop, and I lowered my head beside his neck and urged him on with my knees. He responded with a burst of fresh energy, his mane streaming past my face.

Hast thou clothed his neck in thunder? God had asked Job.

Wasn't God in control even when it didn't seem like it? Who was I to question God? I slowed Red down to a walk, enjoying the crisp morning air. A stream ran along the edge of Uncle Howard's land, and I dismounted at its edge.

The cold wind stung my cheeks, but I ignored the cold and walked closer to the stream.

Momma had said Poppa was drunk when he had entered the burning house. It was hard to believe that Daniel, Michael, and Poppa all drank. Well, I could picture Daniel drinking. But Michael and Poppa? I shook my head.

And, Michael had said someone else. Who had he meant?

My head ached, and I rubbed my temples. If Michael had been talking about Poppa . . . People weren't supposed to speak ill of the dead, were they? Anger surged through me. *How dare he talk about my Poppa!* My head throbbed. Michael was nothing but trouble. I had just been too naive to know it.

But I knew now.

I caught the reins and climbed back on Red. I turned him back toward the stables, and we returned at a walk.

The wind cooled my cheeks, and I felt calmer by the time we reached the barn.

I got the curry comb and gave Red a good brushing before turning my attention to Whitey. He nudged my shoulder with his nose. I rubbed his muzzle, letting the simple act calm me.

Maybe Daniel had not been thinking of me when he bought them. Just the same, I was glad they were here.

I whistled for Chance, and we tussled, and the other dogs joined in. When I tired, I sat cross legged on the ground, and Chance flopped across my lap. I spoke aloud to him.

"Why didn't Michael bring you to me?" He perked his ears toward me.

Clothed In Thunder

Why wasn't Michael the one who now was sober instead of Daniel?

But Chance didn't have the answers. He simply raised his head, striving to understand what I needed. Did I know what I needed myself? Chance gave me what he had, his unconditional love and faithfulness. We sat there as long as the cold would let me before I went in to warm up and eat breakfast.

And so life went on. I had schoolwork, the horses to care for, Chance, and my friends and family. I tried to put Michael out of my mind, but some nights I still cried myself to sleep.

I heard from Daniel—every week. I rarely answered, but the letters kept coming. The letters were friendly, news of his everyday life in the army.

Marla told me she had heard through the grapevine that Michael had moved to Auburn to attend college, just as Laurie had already told me at Christmas. Auburn was just a few miles away, and I couldn't help but think about Michael being so much closer.

I threw myself into my studies, determined to forget him. The days, weeks, and months passed.

By the time school let out for the summer, I was at the top of my class.

Clothed In Thunder

I won several of the class awards, but it was a hollow victory, even when Mr. Albertson presented me with the math award.

Still, it was a victory and held at least a measure of pleasure.

Chapter 18--The Bus Trip

Summer arrived with the days, at first, seeming to stretch endlessly before me. Yet, it came with a change that was to disrupt our lives once again.

Its first indication was Aunt Jenny's letter.

Aunt Jenny wrote to let us know Momma was finally being released. Uncle Colt had gotten her an apartment in town, and she wanted to see Zeke and me.

Uncle Howard and Aunt Liza couldn't get away. Uncle Howard's business had started to pick up, and he needed Aunt Liza's help. They decided we would travel by bus.

It was only June tenth when Zeke and I climbed onto the bus. Even this early in the summer, the temperature climbed to the nineties. At eight o'clock in the morning, it was already sweltering in the packed bus.

I held Zeke on my lap next to the window. A husband and wife, each looking to weigh over two hundred pounds, took up most of the seat, leaving us little room.

Zeke relaxed against me and soon slept, lulled to sleep by the swaying of the bus. I watched the landscape zip by as we traveled. What if Momma asked Zeke and me to move in with her? Or, if she just asked Zeke? What would I do?

I had settled in my new school now and had made friends—Marla and Anne and Andrew. And Uncle Howard and Aunt Liza were so kind to us. My world would have been perfect if not for losing Michael.

Would I be happy leaving Plainsville?

I leaned my head back against the seat and closed my eyes. I grew sticky, wedged against the window with the direct rays of the sun shining through. The hot sun amplified the smell of sweaty bodies. The wind streamed through the opened window, blowing my hair around my face but doing little to cool me off.

Smells of stale tobacco, a baby's dirty diaper, and leather emanating from the seats swirled around me, making me feel nauseous. The baby screamed, only two seats ahead.

Clothed In Thunder

I thought of Cedar Spring. It was always cool there next to the spring flowing over the rocks, underneath the trees that offered abundant shade.

The time Michael and I had sat on the rock, and we had seen the twin fawns was one of my happiest memories. He had kissed me that day. Tears seeped from the corner of my eyes.

I shook my head at myself, willing myself not to think of Michael. Why couldn't I forget him?

Like one of the annoying flies that shared our bus trip, memories of Michael kept returning to me, no matter how much I swatted. I opened my eyes and shifted Zeke to a more comfortable position.

Almost six, he was really too big to be sitting in my lap. He'd start school in the fall. At the thought, my tears flowed faster.

Life changed.

I brushed away my tears. But it wasn't as easy to brush away the uneasiness I felt.

By the time we pulled to the bus stop, my legs had become numb. We were in the middle of the bus and had to wait for everyone to gather their things and shuffle slowly down the aisle.

Uncle Colt waited for us and gave us both a hug. He retrieved our one suitcase before going with Zeke in search of a restroom. As I waited for them near Uncle Colt's wagon, a hand touched me on the shoulder. When I turned, warm brown eyes came into view.

Michael.

He jerked his thumb toward the bus. "I came down on the bus. I'm out of school for the summer."

He'd been on the same bus with me, and I hadn't seen him.

I nodded my head and tried to smile. "Where's your truck?"

"It quit on me. I've been working on it but haven't been able to fix it. I left it in Auburn."

Probably for the best if he was still drinking, and no doubt he was by the way he looked. "How's school going?" I tried to keep my voice light and friendly, but my heart pounded in my ears, and my hands shook.

"Good. I really like it." His cheeks reddened. "You know Sylvia. . ."

My heart leaped in my throat, and I fought to keep the panic at bay. "Yes?" I managed to croak out.

"We've been dating for a couple of months now."

"Great," I forced myself to say. *Why was he torturing me?*

"Are you still planning on being a veterinarian?"

I returned his gaze. Did he think I would just give up on my dreams? Crawl in a hole and die? I threw back my shoulders. "Yes, I am."

He looked relieved. "Well. . .I guess I'll be seeing you around?" His eyes searched mine.

Not if I saw him first. I managed a smile. "Swell."

His eyes saddened. "Listen, Jay, I'm sorry. I just wanted you to know. About Sylvia."

I didn't say anything, only nodded.

"I've got to get going." And with that he left.

Uncle Colt and Zeke returned before I moved from the spot. Uncle Colt placed a hand on the side of the wagon. "That looked like Michael Hutchison."

"It was." I climbed onto the wagon seat, my motions mechanical.

Zeke clambered into the back. He chattered to Uncle Colt as we rode toward the farm. Uncle Colt looked over Zeke's head to study me occasionally, but he didn't speak directly to me until we pulled into the yard.

"Molly's here, waiting for y'all. She's going to spend the night, and I'll take her home in the morning."

That was all he said, but I had a feeling there was more by the way he avoided my eyes. I swiped at Zeke's face and hands with my handkerchief before we climbed off the wagon.

Aunt Jenny, Momma, Laurie, and William all came out to meet us. Zeke ran to Momma, and she knelt to wrap him in an embrace. I hugged everyone and placed a kiss on Momma's cheek. Momma and Zeke led the way into the house.

Aunt Jenny, her arm around my waist, stopped me.

"Anything wrong, Jay?" Her eyes searched me anxiously.

I shrugged my shoulders. "Nothing."

"I know something's wrong. You're not yourself."

Aunt Jenny knew me too well. "Michael has a girlfriend."

"I'm sorry, sweetie."

I shook my head and tried to smile. "It's okay. I should be over him. And, maybe now I finally am."

Yes, Sylvia put the nail in the coffin.

We followed the others into the house.

Chapter 19--Daniel

The delicious smells of Aunt Jenny's cooking filled the house. I went out to the back porch and washed off some of the grime from the long bus ride.

When I went back in, I joined the family already gathered around the table. Aunt Jenny had piled it high with butterbeans, black-eyed peas, fried cornbread, fried chicken, dumplings, fresh sliced tomatoes, and okra.

All foods I would normally have dove into. Now my appetite was gone.

I pretended to eat, toying with my food. Momma, though, was enjoying hers. She still had a pinched, pale complexion from being confined so long, but her face had already begun to fill out, and the dark circles under her eyes had faded since I had seen her at Christmas.

Zeke talked excitedly about our bus trip, getting most things wrong since he slept most of the way. Laurie and William laughed and teased him.

Aunt Jenny and Uncle Colt also talked and laughed. I stayed quiet.

And it wasn't just over Michael. I felt left out, utterly alone. No one talked directly to me. Maybe Aunt Jenny had told them about Michael, and they thought I didn't want to be bothered. But being ignored just increased my sadness.

I had no one. Probably never would. Sure, I had my aunts and uncles, my cousins, my brother. But, somehow, it wasn't enough.

After Zeke ran out of things to tell, Momma turned to face me. "Jay, Colt found me some rooms in town." She looked from me to Uncle Colt.

Uncle Colt nodded. "I've taken over the farm and hired a couple of men to work it. We've managed to make the payments on it so far. Your momma has decided she doesn't want to live there anymore."

My eyes widened in surprise. "You're not going back home?"

Momma shook her head. "I can't make a go of it. I'll never be able to repay Colt for all he's done." Her cheeks reddened. "I had no right to force you and Zeke to work your fingers to the bone."

This new momma I didn't recognize. I continued staring at her until she dropped her eyes.

Everyone had fallen silent, waiting, I thought, to see what I would say. I squirmed in my seat, aware that I should say something to encourage her. "That's okay, Momma."

It was all I could think of to say. It seemed to be enough. Momma raised her eyes and smiled at Aunt Jenny.

"I fixed up the apartment right nice with Jenny's help."

I waited, knowing more was to come.

Momma looked at me, her eyes filled with uncertainty. "I want you and Zeke to move in with me."

I sucked air between my teeth but didn't speak.

"We can come back, Momma?" Zeke scooted from his chair and rushed around the table to throw his arms around her.

Momma lifted Zeke into her lap and brushed his hair back. "If y'all want to." Tears glistened in her eyes.

Zeke's eyes sought mine. "Jay?"

I swallowed the lump in my throat and thought it over. Did Momma really want me back? Or, did she just want Zeke? Did I even want to move back? In a way, it would be better.

Now that Michael was in Auburn, I would be less likely to cross his path if I stayed here. Move back. Resume my old life.

Poppa and the farm gone. *No, not my old life.* My old life was long gone. I searched the faces around me. My cousins, my aunt and uncle. And Zeke. Were they enough to keep me here?

I shrugged my shoulders. "I need to think about it."

Momma didn't argue. "Just take your time. No need to decide today."

"All right." I got up and started clearing the table.

Aunt Jenny shooed me out, telling me to go rest.

It saddened me even more. Aunt Jenny didn't want my help.

What was wrong with me? I knew Aunt Jenny and Uncle Colt loved me. Why, then, did I feel so abandoned?

I ran out of the house and headed to Cedar Spring. What should I do? *Did I belong anywhere?*

If no one wanted me, I would go back to Plainsville. But, could I possibly leave Zeke with Momma? Wasn't he the only one left who really loved me? And, what if she went crazy again, and I lost him?

I followed the trail through the woods down to Cedar Spring. The heat and humidity caused sweat to trickle down my brow.

Clothed In Thunder

It was hard to believe Momma was leaving the farm, moving into town. Then I remembered she came from a large city. She probably wanted to live in town.

Not me. I wanted to live back on the farm, back to where I once lived with Poppa, the place where I once felt love.

Would I ever be able to live on the farm again? Uncle Colt was paying the mortgage. Didn't that mean the farm was his? I would never be able to pay him back, even if one day he agreed to sell it back to me.

I sat on a rock and let my hand trail into the cool stream, still as confused as ever. Tadpoles swam close to the edge, many already with legs emerging. I thought of the frog in the cream, swimming around and around. Wasn't that what I had been doing? But where had it gotten me? I still drowned, only now sucked into the butter, unable to move on.

A twig snapped, and I raised my head.

Daniel stood at the edge of the clearing.

A smile spread across his face when he saw me look up. He walked to me, and I watched him approach.

"Hey, Jay. I didn't know you were here."

"I didn't know you were either." I moved over on the rock to allow him to sit beside me.

"Decided to use my weekend pass to come visit the old home place," he said.

I nodded. "We came to see Momma. She was released from the hospital a few days ago." How much did he know about Momma? It wasn't a secret how she had acted after Poppa died.

"That's great news. Is she doing okay?"

"Yeah." I looked down at my hands, trying to sort through my feelings. For some reason, Dan sitting next to me didn't feel awkward at all. What was wrong with me? Too much on my mind to care anymore?

I turned to face him. "She wants me to move back."

"You don't sound too happy about it." His gentle voice persuaded me to continue.

"I don't know what to do. She wants me and Zeke to move to a place in town."

"Oh. Not back to the farm?"

"No. Uncle Colt has taken over the farm." It hurt to say the words. I knew Uncle Colt couldn't be expected to make payments for no telling how long, and then give it back to me. It wouldn't be fair to him.

"I know that must be difficult for you."

"It's okay." I waved a hand in dismissal of the farm, although its loss, I knew, would forever haunt me. I lifted my head to look into his eyes of hazel. "I don't know what to do about Zeke. I can't leave him here, can I?"

"I don't know." His eyes clouded. "Do you want to move back?"

"I want to go to college. Become a veterinarian. If I move back. . ."

"You're not sure if you would ever fulfill your dream?" Daniel watched me, his eyes compassionate.

"Yes. But I don't know what Momma might do. She could go crazy again like she did before." I chewed my lip.

"People can change, Jay."

I searched his eyes. The way he said it made me wonder if he spoke of Momma or himself. "But what if she goes back to the way she was?"

A kind smile spread across his face. "Sometimes you just have to have faith in people."

Did he mean I should have faith in him? "It's hard when they've hurt you." And, I didn't know if I meant Momma or him.

"Jay, *what do you want?*"

His question startled me. "What do you mean?"

"Do you want to stay here or in Plainsville? Forget about Zeke for a moment. *What do you want?*"

"I want to stay in Plainsville," I said without hesitation.

"Stay there, then. Your aunt and uncle are nearby in case anything happens. They would watch out for Zeke."

I slid off the rock and moved a few feet away. I studied him, and he allowed me, not showing the least embarrassment. He met my gaze undisturbed.

I saw that Sylvia was right. Daniel wore a short-sleeve shirt and looked fit and tan. He had never looked better.

Daniel came to me, and I stayed rooted to the spot. He gazed at me with . . . with such tenderness that I realized Michael was right, too. Daniel loved me.

Chapter 20--Daniel's Friendship

J licked my lips. "I saw Michael. He was on the bus, and he told me he was dating Sylvia." I blurted it out without thought.

He nodded his head, his eyes still tender. Suddenly, without knowing how, my head lay on his shoulder, and he wrapped his arms around me.

I struggled but tears came. I cried until I hiccupped. He stroked my hair, making shushing noises, yet the tears still came.

"I've tried to talk to Michael," he said.

"What?" His voice sounded far away. I straightened and tried to staunch the tears, to understand what he was saying.

"I've tried to talk to him. You see it's my fault."

"What do you mean?"

"It's my fault he drinks. We started when we were very young--we were in sixth grade. I snuck a bottle of whiskey out of my house. That's the first time we got drunk." He pulled out his handkerchief and offered it to me.

I took it and swiped at the tears. "Yes, Michael told me he started drinking when he was young. Your parents didn't know?"

He stared into the distance. "My father may have known. I don't think he cared. My mother had already died by then."

My conscience pricked me. I had never thought about Daniel's relationship with his father. Never even thought about the death of his mother.

"Michael and I--sometimes others, like William--would sneak whiskey from my father. Sometimes we would buy whiskey, moonshine, whatever we could get our hands on."

"My cousin William?" Was that who Michael had meant when he accused someone in my family of being a drunk? Was it William?

"William only went with us a couple of times then he stopped. I think maybe your uncle caught him." He gave a slight grimace. "If we'd all been lucky enough to have fathers who cared. . ."

I let out a sigh of relief--no, it wasn't William. "Michael's father didn't care?" I had always thought he seemed like a nice man. Did Michael have problems I knew nothing of? How selfish I had been--not noticing others struggled just as I did. Maybe more.

"I don't know. Maybe he never found out." He shrugged. "Sometimes we'd take the whiskey to school in our lunchboxes."

I nodded my head, thinking about how the older boys were always so chummy at recess and the lunch period. "And the teachers didn't know?"

He shrugged his shoulders. "If they did, they never said anything."

"What made you quit?"

"After I joined the army, I kept drinking. But it only got me into more and more trouble. One of my army buddies told me about this new group--Alcoholics Anonymous. I started going to the meetings. It's been a struggle, but with the help of those going through the same thing, somehow it's easier."

"Yes, I think it would be."

"And one of the steps is to make amends to those we have wronged. Michael was the first one I thought of. It's my fault he's an alcoholic."

I felt sick to my stomach. "You think Michael is an alcoholic?"

"Michael always drank more than I did. He pretty much lived on the verge of drunkenness every single day." He looked at me solemnly. "Still does."

This was hard for me to comprehend. I shook my head again. "How would I not know? How can he hide it?"

"He's one of those who can hold their liquor. And, he's good at hiding it. They learn to keep a distance between themselves and others." He shrugged his shoulders. "There's different ways of hiding it."

I looked at him doubtfully, not sure how I could have missed the signs, no matter what Daniel told me. "So what happened when you talked to Michael?"

"He wouldn't listen. He said his drinking was under control. I told him about AA, and he said it was all a bunch of nonsense. Said his drinking was no big deal."

"Yes, he said that to me, too."

"I told him he needed to be honest with you."

"When? On that day when he was so angry? When he brought the horses? Did you tell him then?"

"Yes. I'm sorry." He sighed heavily. "I didn't know he would react that way."

"It's not your fault." I suddenly realized Daniel still held me in his arms. I pushed gently away. "I'd better get going. I wanted to go by the farm."

Daniel didn't immediately release me. "Can I come with you?" His voice was a soft whisper in my ear.

I hesitated then nodded my head. "Sure." My emotions were in a turmoil.

He released me, and I led the way from the clearing, wondering why I had let him come with me.

His arms had offered such comfort. He really did seem to care. Maybe I could learn to care for him in the same way, if I would only allow myself.

We walked without speaking until we came to the farm. He hung back, allowing me to wander down to the barn and around the house. The house was locked. I'd have to ask Uncle Colt for a key if I wanted to go in. But, I wasn't sure if I needed to.

I looked into the windows and saw most of the furniture had been removed. Momma had taken it to furnish the apartment, I supposed. No, it was not my home now. If I went inside, that would just make it all the more painfully clear.

I was aware Daniel's eyes followed me although he still kept his distance. I walked slowly back to him.

He held out a hand to me. "I can help you, Jay."

I didn't take his hand. It was too soon.

He let his hand fall to his side. "Will you let me?"

I searched his eyes. "I don't know."

He didn't seem angry but smiled. Was he just happy I hadn't said no?

I allowed him to walk me back to Aunt Jenny's house. He asked if he could see me again. I nodded my assent, and he left without coming in.

Aunt Jenny was the only one at the house when I got back. Her anxious eyes surveyed me. "We were getting worried about you."

I waved a hand at her. "I'm okay, Aunt Jenny."

Relief washed over her face. She motioned me to sit, and I obeyed.

"Do you want a cup of coffee? Just made some fresh."

"Yes, please."

She poured us each a cup and brought them to the table.

"Where is everyone?" I asked.

"They all went into town with Molly. Your uncle will take you later. I wanted to talk to you first."

I waited for her to continue.

"Your uncle and I think you should go back to Plainsville and leave Zeke here. He's young and needs to be with his mother."

I saw the surprise on her face when I nodded my head. "She seems changed. I know you and

Uncle Colt will be there for Zeke if he needs you."

"You know we will. And, if we see there's a problem, we'll let you know."

I took a sip of the strong, black coffee. "I wish I could be sure she's really changed. . ."

"Sometimes we just have to trust people, Jay. And, trust God."

Just what Daniel had said. I nodded my head. "I know."

Aunt Jenny looked at me steadily. "Your uncle and I want you to finish high school, go on to college." She took my hand in hers. "Jay, do what you dream of. We can't live others' lives for them. Zeke has his own life."

"But, Aunt Jenny, if I don't stay with Zeke, aren't I being selfish?"

"No. Preparing for your future is not selfish. Zeke will be fine."

"I'll just have to trust that he will be." I finished my coffee, wondering if my trust would be strong enough.

"You'll see. God's plans are much better than any we can come up with. He's got great things in store for you." She pushed back from the table. "Want to go to the garden with me?"

"Sure." Daniel and Aunt Jenny had helped me realize the path I needed to choose. Life consisted of losses. To get through it, I would just have to trust God. And people.

Yet, the pain of losing Poppa, Michael, and now Zeke threatened to tear my soul in two. Daniel seemed ready to help me through this new loss. *Who would've thought?*

Shaking my head at the mystery of God, I followed Aunt Jenny out to the garden.

Chapter 21--Telling Momma

Uncle Colt took me into town on the wagon and dropped me off at a house that had been divided in half to make two apartments. Momma's was the one on the right, Uncle Colt had told me.

I headed up the wooden steps. I barely knocked when Zeke opened the door and threw his arms around me.

The apartment consisted of a large front room, two small bedrooms, and a tiny kitchen. Zeke ran around the small space, showing me every inch. A backdoor led from the kitchen to a porch area. A bathroom had been built on one end of the porch to be shared by both apartments.

Momma smiled, her eyes shining. She ushered me to a couch in the front room. Zeke climbed up beside me while Momma settled into the rocking chair, the one from our old house. *The one she rocked so hard whenever she became upset.* Now, the rockers simply bumped the floor gently.

Momma scrutinized me. "You've changed," she said.

She was right. I had. I nodded my head.

She smiled. "I've got a job, Sarah Jane."

"That's good. Where at?"

"I'm working at the ten cent store up the street. It's an easy walk from here."

"Great."

She kept watching me closely. "I want you and Zeke to come live with me. You could help out, Sarah Jane. Someone needs to watch Zeke while I work. When he starts to school in the fall, someone will need to take him and pick him up."

I squirmed uneasily. "Momma. . ." I looked at Zeke. I needed to talk to him first before I told her. "Momma, Zeke hasn't shown me the backyard."

Zeke leaped from the couch. "Come on, Jay."

I allowed him to lead me into the yard.

A young boy who appeared to be about his age dug into the dirt by the house with an old spoon.

He peered up at us. "Hi, Zeke."

Clothed In Thunder

"Hey, Lamar! This is my sister, Jay." Zeke grinned, glancing from his new friend to me. "Lamar lives next door."

The young boy held up a wiggling worm. "I'm getting us some bait for fishing."

"I'll help you," Zeke said, about to fall to his knees to dig in the dark dirt.

I lifted him by his elbow. "Wait, Zeke. I wanted to talk to you first."

Zeke looked at me in dismay. "Now?"

"Yes, now." I wanted to get this over with as soon as possible.

"All right. I'll be back, Lamar," he promised. We walked around the corner of the house to a side yard. An oak tree shaded a small bench, and we sat down.

"Zeke, do you want to live here?" I waited for his response although I already knew what it would be.

A smile spread over his face. "Yes! Lamar told me his big brother is gonna take us fishing." He tilted his head and looked at me, frowning slightly. "If we get enough worms." He squirmed, and I knew he would blame me if they didn't.

I nodded. "It sounds like you'll have a lot of fun living here."

"*We'll* have a lot of fun," he corrected me. "I bet Lamar's brother will let you come fishing with us."

"I'm not staying, Zeke. I'm going back to Plainsville."

His forehead furrowed. "Going back?"

"I want to finish high school. You know I want to be a veterinarian. There's a college near Plainsville where I can go to become one." A lump formed in my throat. "But Momma wants you to stay here."

"Without you?" The creases deepened.

"Yes, without me. You'll have Momma. And Lamar. And you'll make more friends."

"Jay, I don't want to stay here without you. What if Momma . . ." His eyes widened as if he relived an old memory.

"She's better, Zeke. Besides, Uncle Colt and Aunt Jenny will watch out for you." I hugged him to me. "If you need me, just tell them, and I'll come back."

"Promise?"

"I promise." I kept my arms wrapped around him until he began to squirm again.

"Jay, can I go look for worms now?"

"Sure."

He leaped up from the bench and scampered around the edge of the house. A sharp pain pierced my heart. He'd forget me. He'd half forgotten me now in the joy of making a new friend.

Yes, people changed. Zeke was growing up. Yet, worry still gnawed me. What if Momma began acting strange again? And I wasn't here to protect him? Was it wrong for me to leave him when I might be putting him in danger?

Clothed In Thunder

I followed Zeke back to the backyard and watched for a moment as he extracted the wigglers from the ground, his face full of laughter. I left Zeke digging worms and went back inside.

Momma, in the kitchen, pointed to the icebox. "You thirsty, Sarah Jane? I'll make us a glass of iced tea."

"Yes, ma'am," I said. It felt strange for Momma to be waiting on me. I resisted the urge to do it myself.

Momma and I settled back in the front room with our glasses of tea. The house had been built to take advantage of even a hint of a breeze. With all the windows opened, the wind made the curtains flutter.

I liked the house. I felt comfortable here. Surely, Zeke would be happy here.

I took a sip of the iced tea before speaking. "Momma, I'm not staying."

"Why?" She didn't look angry, only curious.

"I want to finish school and go to college."

"I just don't understand you, Sarah Jane. Women don't need education. They just need to find a good man."

"Were you raised that way, to believe women do not need to be educated?"

She stared at the wall behind my head for a long minute before her eyes refocused on me. "My mother raised me to catch a husband. A wealthy one if I could."

"Really?" I asked, curious about her upbringing, trying to see her with new eyes.

"My family wasn't rich, but we weren't poor. My father had a good job. I was an only child, and my mother had big plans for me." She closed her eyes for a moment.

"Where are your parents now?"

"Dead. They both died before I met your father." She took a sip of tea. "Yes, I was taught a good marriage is all you need to be happy."

"Momma, I want more." I had told her this before. Did she remember?

She slowly shook her head at me. "I don't understand that. I guess I've never really understood you, Sarah Jane."

"I've wanted to be a veterinarian for as long as I can remember." I hesitated. "I could stay here for a while, until Zeke settles in."

Momma shook her head. "No, go on back. I don't want to keep you from doing what you want. I'm sure I can find someone to take Zeke to school."

Did she really mean that? Or, did she simply want to get rid of me? I studied her face. Could she really have changed so much? She didn't seem angry, only sad, the corners of her lips slightly drooping.

I rose and kissed her cheek. "Thank you, Momma."

Chapter 22--Trip with Daniel

J slept on the couch and Zeke in his new room. After breakfast, Zeke and I went for a walk to see his new school, only three blocks from the apartment. I sighed with relief that it was such a short distance.

When we arrived back, Daniel waited on the front porch. Zeke barely said hello before running to the backyard to find Lamar.

"Well?" Daniel asked when Zeke had gone.

"Zeke's staying. I'm going back to Plainsville." I shuffled my feet, slightly at unease when I remembered crying on his shoulder.

"Let's walk over to the drugstore. I'll buy you a malt."

I hesitated for just a second. "Let me tell Momma."

I opened the door and stuck my head in. "I'll be back in a little while. Zeke's in the yard."

"All right," she called back.

When I closed the door, Daniel held out his hand. This time, I didn't hesitate but threaded my fingers through his. We walked in silence, hand in hand.

At the drugstore, we found a booth empty in the back corner.

After Daniel ordered our malts, he gave me an encouraging smile. "I think you're doing the right thing."

"I hope so."

"I'll come see you when I can."

I nodded my head.

"When are you leaving?" He reached across the table to recapture my hand.

"Monday. That reminds me. I've got to go turn in Zeke's bus ticket."

"Why don't you turn in yours, too? I can take you back."

The malts arrived, and he released my hand. *My first malt.* I drank half of it before I answered. "Sure. If it's not any trouble. . ."

"No, I'm going back to camp on Monday, and it's on my way." He watched me drain the rest of the malt, a smile playing on his lips. "Good?"

"Delicious. Umm. . .how do you like the army?"

"To tell you the truth, basic almost killed me. The drill sergeant was always in our faces, screaming." He grinned at me. "I have a bad habit of putting my hands in my pockets. The drill sergeant had chewed me out a couple of times when I did it again. He told me to go find two BRs."

"BRs? What's a BR?"

"Exactly. I had no idea. Finally, after I had searched around for a while, he screamed 'Big Rocks!' He added a few colorful words that I won't repeat. I had to carry huge rocks in my pockets for three days."

I laughed, and his face lit up. "It's good to hear you laugh. Even if it is about me."

I laughed again. "Sounds like the army's pretty tough."

"That was basic. Now, things are much better."

"I'm glad." And I truly was.

"Another malt?" he asked.

Was I being too greedy? I didn't care. "Sure."

And he chuckled before ordering me another one.

Momma agreed to let Daniel drive me back to Plainsville. Leaving wasn't as hard as I thought it would be. Daniel promised Zeke he would bring me back to visit whenever he could, and Zeke seemed satisfied with that.

The trip back to Aunt Liza and Uncle Howard's flew by with Daniel keeping me entertained with more stories about the army.

Chance greeted me, his entire body undulating with each wag of his tail. Daniel and I spent a moment with him before going in.

Aunt Liza and Uncle Howard, expecting me back later on the bus, looked up in surprise when we came into the sitting room.

Uncle Howard's face, dark as a thundercloud, didn't clear when he saw us. After a moment, he made a visible effort to speak to Daniel in a normal voice. Aunt Liza's eyes looked as if she had been crying. What in the world had happened while I was gone?

"You're early," Aunt Liza said. It sounded like an accusation.

I indicated Daniel. "He offered to drive me home, so I wouldn't have to ride the bus."

She nodded listlessly, not even making an effort to be civil.

"Where's Zeke?" Uncle Howard asked.

"Momma's much better. Zeke stayed with her," I said.

Aunt Liza's head snapped up. "He's not coming back? You left him?" Her eyes filled with tears.

I glanced at Daniel, feeling uncertain again, and he nodded his encouragement.

"Momma's living in town now and has a job. Zeke wanted to stay."

"I'm sure Jenny and Colt know how to watch out for Zeke," Uncle Howard said forcefully.

His face darkened even more, and I licked my lips, afraid of this side of my uncle I had never seen. "Yes, they promised me they would. I'm sure he'll be okay."

Aunt Liza nodded her head, squeezed her eyes tight, and bowed her head.

Daniel looked uncertain for a second. "I've got to be going. It was good seeing y'all again." He shook Uncle Howard's hand.

Aunt Liza didn't respond.

Daniel's eyes filled with concern when I walked out with him. "I hate to leave you. . ."

I shook my head. "It'll be all right. They probably just had a little argument. All couples argue sometimes, don't they?"

"I suppose." He leaned back against the car, folding his arms. "It seems more than a simple argument."

"Maybe she burnt the biscuits?" I spoke lightly.

He chuckled. "Yeah, maybe something that simple." He pushed away from the car and faced me. "Let me know if you need me? Promise?"

"I promise." After all, who else did I have?

He kissed my forehead, and I watched him leave, knowing I would miss him.

Or, at least miss the malts. I laughed at myself and went into the house.

Aunt Liza had retreated to the kitchen and had poured herself a cup of coffee.

"Where's Uncle Howard?"

"He went out to his shop."

I joined her at the table. "What's wrong with him, Aunt Liza?"

"I reckon Howard's upset about Zeke." Aunt Liza shook her head sadly. "We're going to miss that young'n."

"No, he was angry when we came in. Something else is wrong."

She sighed heavily and averted her eyes. "Howard lost the job."

"Oh, no! What happened?"

She shrugged her shoulders and stared into her coffee cup. "I don't want to talk about it now."

I walked over and hugged her. "All right. But let me know if you need to talk."

She simply nodded, and I left her nursing her coffee.

I walked to the barn, led Red out, and saddled him.

Did Uncle Howard lose the job because he had been drinking? Could he be the one Michael meant? If he was losing jobs because of drinking, maybe I should talk to him or Aunt Liza, tell them of Alcoholics Anonymous. But, what if I was wrong?

And, really, was it any of my business?

Clothed In Thunder

At any rate, I needed to find work. I had been a financial burden long enough. I swung into the saddle, resolving to help my aunt and uncle. Maybe Marla's father would be able to find me a job.

I decided to go see him first thing tomorrow.

Chapter 23--Michael & Sylvia

Marla's father only knew of a babysitting job. One of his friends owned a florist shop, and his wife helped part time with the bookkeeping. I would work only three days a week, in the afternoons.

But at least it was a job, and one I liked. The two boys were six and four. The oldest helped ease my loneliness for Zeke. The youngest was always into mischief. He kept me from dwelling too much on my troubles.

Troubles that now seemed to be receding, even though I missed Zeke. Marla and I spent as much time together as we could.

Her aunt left Marla a small sum of money, and she used it for braces. Whenever she smiled, the gold in her mouth flashed, even in the dimmest of light.

Sylvia kept her distance, and I heard no more from Michael. I assumed he was in Auburn, but here in Plainsville I never saw him. And, that was a relief.

And there was Daniel. His camp was close enough that I saw him often. We'd spend Saturdays riding horses, playing with Chance, and taking in afternoon matinees. Of course, I missed Zeke, but Momma and Aunt Jenny wrote often, and I knew he was flourishing.

So life went on. Then, one summer night, to celebrate my sixteenth birthday, Daniel asked me to go with him to dinner and a picture show in the large city near his camp. He thought we should make a party of it by inviting my friends.

Marla now had a boyfriend, Andrew, and they both were eager to go. Andrew's sister Anne, not wanting to be left out, made Andrew fix her up with one of his friends, a boy I didn't know named Tommy.

When we arrived at the theater, Daniel insisted on paying for everyone's admission, amidst their half-hearted protests.

We settled into our seats and chatted about his horses as we waited for the movie to begin. The theater darkened, and he reached for my hand, his grasp, warm and strong.

I barely concentrated on the movie, thinking about his nearness in the dark. I tightened my fingers around his, and he gently squeezed my hand.

Katharine Hepburn and Cary Grant couldn't distract me from my thoughts. What I had felt for Michael had been a fantasy. Daniel was reality--kind, strong, and reassuring. The army had changed him, the army and AA. And, I was thankful. I didn't know how I could have gotten through the last month or two without him.

After the movie, we headed for a diner. Although crowded, we found a table against the back wall to fit all of us. Daniel pulled his chair close to mine and put an arm across the back, letting his hand drape along my shoulder.

"I can't believe that show," Andrew said, shaking his head.

"What do you mean?" Anne asked.

"The whole thing was just crazy. A leopard named Baby."

Tommy nodded. "And a circus just happens to be in town, and a wild leopard just happens to escape."

"Unbelievable," Andrew said.

"Cary Grant is dreamy," Anne said. "That makes up for all the plot problems."

Marla and I nodded our heads in agreement.

Tommy curled his lips into a look of disgust. "Dreamy in a . . . what do you call it?" Tommy asked.

"Negligee." Anne smiled at him. "He's dreamy in whatever he's wearing."

The boys and Daniel laughed, shaking their heads. A pretty waitress came to the table, a pencil stuck behind one ear.

"What'll it be?" She had a bored expression on her face until she saw Daniel. Her eyes brightened as she looked directly at him.

I felt a pang of jealousy.

"Six milkshakes. Three chocolate, two vanilla, and one strawberry," Daniel said.

"Yes, sir." She smiled as she walked away.

Andrew punched Tommy's arm. "Uniforms sure get attention. I'm joining the army as soon as I graduate."

Anne frowned at her brother. "You need good looks if you want attention like Daniel gets. And you're a little . . . short in that department."

Daniel's cheeks reddened as much as Andrew's as the rest of us laughed. I turned my head, not wanting to embarrass him more. The door of the diner swung open.

Michael and Sylvia walked in.

My mouth fell open, and Marla turned to follow my gaze.

"There's Sylvia," she said, in surprise.

Everyone turned to look.

"Wow. That fellow she's with is better looking than Cary Grant!" Anne said.

The color in Daniel's face deepened, and he frowned briefly. Then he smoothed his forehead and straightened his shoulders.

"Michael!" Daniel called.

My head snapped up. Why would he call Michael over here? Warmth flooded my cheeks, yet, I couldn't tear my eyes away as Michael walked toward our table, Sylvia clutching his arm. Michael smiled easily, his eyes sweeping the table.

"Care to join us?" Daniel asked.

I looked at Daniel in amazement. Why would he invite Michael to sit with us? I shifted uncomfortably in my seat. Surely Michael would decline. But, no, he held a chair out for Sylvia and sat down at the end of the table next to Daniel.

"Hi, Jay." Michael grinned at me.

"Hi," I croaked. What was wrong with me? I was over him, wasn't I? Daniel was worth ten of him. But my heart wouldn't accept what my head knew.

Daniel made the introductions while my heart beat erratically. I chewed on my bottom lip and let my gaze fall to my hands. Michael. With Sylvia. How could I bear it? I tried to chide myself. Wasn't I just thinking Daniel was so much better than Michael? And, now, I was a trembling mass of emotion.

Daniel chatted easily with Michael, asking how college was going.

Michael shook his head. "Reckon it could be better. How's the army treating you?"

Without hearing the answer, I stood and Daniel and Michael rose at the same time. Tommy and Andrew hesitated a second before following their leads.

"Um . . . I need to powder my nose." Blindly, I escaped from the table and stumbled toward the restroom.

I heard chairs scraping, and Marla and Anne caught up with me.

"Is Sylvia coming, too?" I whispered.

Marla shook her head. I headed to the sink and leaned against it.

"How do you know Michael?" Anne asked, curiosity brimming in her eyes.

I had never told anyone about Michael except Marla. I couldn't answer, still leaning on the sink for support.

"She used to date him," Marla answered for me.

"Wow. You've dated two of the best-looking guys I've ever seen." Anne looked at me as if she'd never really seen me before.

Marla was indignant. "Why are you surprised? Jay is beautiful and smart."

"I didn't say she wasn't," Anne said. "I'm sorry, Jay, if I offended you."

I waved my hand. "No, you didn't offend me. Don't worry about it."

"I don't know who's better looking, Michael or Daniel," Anne said.

"Michael," I said automatically. I clamped a hand over my mouth and shook my head.

Marla and Anne exchanged looks.

"I'm sorry," I said. "I mean Daniel." To my consternation, I burst out crying.

Marla had her arm around me, patting my back. "Oh, Jay! Bless your heart."

Anne, too, joined her. "Jay, don't let Michael get you down. Daniel's a wonderful guy."

My crying slowed, and I sniffled. "I know he is." But he wasn't Michael, was he?

"Come on, Jay. You don't want him to see you like this, do you?" Anne peered into my face anxiously.

Which one, I thought? "No." I turned to the sink and splashed water on my face.

Marla opened her purse and pulled out a compact. I stood compliant while she powdered my face. I had a lipstick in my pocket, applied a little, and blotted my lips.

Marla nodded her approval. "They're going to be wondering where we are. Are you going to be okay, Jay?"

I nodded my head and squared my shoulders. I'd show him. I plastered a smile on my face and followed them out.

Chapter 24--Not Michael

J slid into my seat next to Daniel. He turned anxious eyes on me and smiled. I guess I appeared calm enough. He leaned back in his chair and wrapped his arm again around my shoulders.

I caught his hand in mine and leaned closer to him, pretending to ignore Michael.

But I was acutely aware of him, aware of his every move. My stomach did flip flops.

"How's Zeke?" Michael asked.

I glanced in his direction but couldn't quite meet his eyes. "He's doing fine. He wrote a letter to me the other day."

"Wrote a letter?" Michael frowned.

"Yes. He's back home, living with Momma."

"Oh, I hadn't heard."

I forced a smile on my face. "Yes. He'll start first grade in the fall."

"He's not even in first grade, and he wrote a letter to you?" Marla asked.

"Yes," I said proudly. "Momma said he may even skip first grade and go into second."

"He might be as smart as his big sister," Andrew said.

"He'd have to be mighty smart," Marla said. "Jay had the highest grade point average in our class." She cast a glance at Michael as if letting him know what he had missed out on.

Sylvia propped her elbows on the table and rested her chin on her hands, looking at me steadily. I looked back with what I hoped was a look of indifference.

"Yes, she's always been at the top of her class," Michael said.

I glanced at him through my lashes. He looked at me intently, and my heart thundered in my chest, no matter how much I willed it not to.

Sylvia tittered. "Not when she first got here." She glanced around the table as if daring anyone to contradict her. "She was at the bottom of Mr. Albertson's class."

Daniel squeezed my shoulders. "Jay's always been the smartest and the prettiest girl around in my book."

"Stop. You're embarrassing me." I picked up my milkshake and took a sip.

"I admire all you've done when I know you must have been worried sick with your mother in a sanatorium," Sylvia said.

I gasped and struggled to my feet, not upset at her words, but at the realization that *Michael had talked to her about me.* "Let's go, Daniel."

I stumbled toward the door, not caring if anyone followed. I made it out before a hand grabbed me and twirled me around.

"Jay. . ." Michael's face was pinched and white.

Daniel, behind him, balled his hands into fists. "Get your hands off her."

Michael released me and stepped back. Daniel put his arm around my waist. We walked away, and I glanced over my shoulder. Sylvia joined Michael on the sidewalk.

"Did I say something wrong?" She widened her eyes as she peered up into Michael's face.

Michael didn't reply. I turned away and hurried across the parking lot.

Daniel and I climbed in the car and waited for the others, neither of us speaking. When the others silently climbed in, Daniel cranked the car and drove away.

I sat up front between Daniel and Marla, gradually calming down. I finally laughed. "Sylvia's right."

No one answered.

I twisted in my seat to scan the faces shrouded in the dark. "My momma was mentally ill." I didn't tell them she was my stepmother. She *was* the only mother I had ever known. "She was recently released from a psychiatric ward. It's not a secret. I'm sorry I got upset. I shouldn't have." I shrugged my shoulders.

Daniel hit the steering wheel with the heel of his hand. "Michael had no business telling Sylvia about your mother. Why did I call them over to the table?"

"I don't know. Why did you?" I waited for his answer.

He cleared his throat. "Mike's always been a good friend of mine. You know I've been trying to help him." He gave me a sideways glance.

"Help how?" Anne asked.

"Michael drinks," I said softly.

Andrew snorted. "Lots of guys drink."

Daniel shook his head darkly. "Not like Michael. He needs help. Probably why he's been saying things he shouldn't."

"Some people just don't want to be helped," I said.

"If I had known Michael told Sylvia about your mother. . ."

"It doesn't matter. Everyone at home knows. Why shouldn't people here?"

Marla patted my arm. "I'm sorry, Jay."

"Really, it's okay. Should I be ashamed of my mother?"

"Of course you shouldn't be," Anne said. "We're not supposed to hurt others. Sylvia sits in church every single Sunday and then acts like that, all innocent but trying to upset you."

"Enough about me. Let's talk about something else. Please?"

Marla and Anne hesitated only a moment before they obeyed and talked again of the movie. Eventually, I joined in, firmly blocking Michael and Sylvia from my mind, wishing my heart had not betrayed me.

After we dropped everyone off, I still stayed next to Daniel. He parked in the yard, and we remained as we were. I lay my head on his shoulder, trying to recapture the feeling I had had just a few short hours ago as we sat in the darkened theater. Why wasn't Daniel enough? Why couldn't I get over Michael?

I sighed and straightened. "I'd better be getting in."

He opened the door, slid out, and took my hand to help me. We walked to the house through the darkness. Only a sliver of a moon hung in the sky.

"I'm going back to camp tonight."

"When will you be back?"

"Probably not until next month." He raised my hand to his lips.

When I didn't protest, he pulled me closer and gently brushed my lips with his.

He pulled back and cupped my chin in his hand. "I'll miss you."

"I'll miss you, too," I said.

He kissed me again before he released me. He waited until I stepped through the door and closed it. I leaned with my back against it and touched my lips with my fingertips.

No matter how much I wanted him to be, he was not Michael. But he was still a good man. And a pretty good kisser to boot.

I smiled and tiptoed quietly to bed.

Chapter 25--An Opportunity

Principal Martin nodded to my aunt and uncle. "I wanted to let you know Alabama Polytechnic Institute is offering your niece a special opportunity. Based on her grades and test scores, they are going to allow her to take classes this fall. If she does well, she can continue. Of course, if she doesn't, she'll have to reenroll in high school."

I looked at him in astonishment. "You mean I'm not going back to high school, sir?"

Principal Martin perched on the edge of the couch. He looked around at our faces and smiled. "That's right. As long as you maintain a B average this fall at API, you will be officially graduated from high school."

Uncle Howard and Aunt Liza beamed at me. But I wasn't sure if this was what I wanted. Going to college meant I would have a greater chance to run into Michael. And, did I want to leave my friends behind and not graduate with my class?

"Yes," he continued. "You'll receive a scholarship to pay your tuition. The scholarship won't cover all your expenses, such as your books."

"Jay has a part-time job," Uncle Howard said.

Principal Martin looked dubious. "The degree she has chosen to pursue is a tough one. If she graduates, she'll be one of the first female veterinarians ever to graduate from API."

"One of the first?" Aunt Liza's face radiated delight. "I know she can do it."

"It'll be difficult, especially if she continues to work at this job." He appraised me.

I met his eyes. "Sir, my job is only a few hours a week. I'm sure I can do it." But did I want to? Was I really sure I could?

He nodded his head at me, his eyes thoughtful. Then he smiled. "I'm sure you can."

He took his leave, and, as soon as he drove away, Aunt Liza squealed like a school girl. Uncle Howard gave me a bear hug.

Although I shared their excitement, fear coursed through me. I didn't want to leave my friends. The high school, once so large and gloomy, seemed now like a haven, a cozy retreat compared to the sprawling campus right in the next town. I didn't have to accept the offer, did I? But right now, my aunt and uncle were much too excited for me to discuss it with them.

I had to talk to someone, so I walked over to Marla's, calling Chance to follow me. I didn't tell her the news until we went into the front parlor. She squealed in delight just as Aunt Liza had done.

"Shhh...," I cautioned.

"Why?" Her brows drew together in puzzlement.

"I'm not sure if I want to go."

"Are you crazy? Of course you want to go."

I got up and walked around the room. "I want to go, but I don't want to leave you and Anne. Even Andrew and Tommy. . ."

"We can still see each other after school and on weekends."

I wrung my hands and continued my pacing. "But what if I can't do the work. . ."

"Jay, you can do it. You need to believe in yourself. Look how far you've come since you've been here."

I took a seat by her and searched her eyes. "Michael. . .What if I see him?" If I were really truthful with myself, Michael was at the root of my fear.

"Pshaw! Just ignore him." She shook her head at me. "Are you ever going to forget him? If Daniel can't take his place in your heart, I don't know who could."

"I know Daniel's a great guy. I know that. . ." I looked down at my hands clasped in my lap, wishing with all my heart that he meant more to me than Michael. Maybe one day he would--it just wasn't today. I sighed.

"Jay, API is a big place. You'll probably never see Michael. And, so what if you do?"

"I know you're right. And, even if I can ignore him, I'll still miss all of y'all. Especially you, Marla."

"This is a wonderful opportunity for you."

"Okay," I said doubtfully. "Maybe I can do it. And, if I get sent back to high school, it won't be the first time I'll be sent back to a lower grade."

"Great! I'm sure you'll do fine. Now let's go tell the rest of the gang."

"All right." I got to my feet, my shoulders sagging.

Marla took me by the shoulders and gave me a shake. "Jay! Act happy!"

And, I truly tried, but dread dogged my steps. And dread was named Michael.

I gave Aunt Liza a peck on the cheek the first morning of classes. I barely made it in time to catch the bus that would take me to the college.

Clothed In Thunder

Once seated on the bus, I took a deep breath. I could do this.

I had made a map of the campus and labeled each class and room number on it. Maybe it would keep me from getting lost.

My palms were sweaty, and I rubbed them against my dress. The sweltering bus ride left me sticky, so that by the time the bus reached campus, my dress clung to me.

At least my legs were bare, except for my socks at my ankles, and that helped keep me somewhat cooler. I felt strange with bare legs, but all the other girls wore similar shoes and socks, so I fit right in.

I was part of a dozen or so students who disembarked. I stood for a moment, looking around. I pulled out my sketch, marked with my classes and times. I studied it but could make no sense of what I had drawn.

A voice spoke in my ear. "Lost?"

I turned to face Michael, dismayed to see him so soon. I tried to smooth the planes of my face.

"Not yet." I tried to keep my voice calm.

"You mean you're taking classes here?" He took the sketch from my hands.

"Yes. At least for now."

He kept watching me.

"If you must know, I received a special scholarship. If I keep my grades up, I'm here to stay." I held my hand out to take my sketch back, but, to my annoyance, he stuffed it in his pocket.

"So happens my first class is in the same building. I'll walk with you." He didn't look at me, just started striding away.

I hurried to keep up with him, angry, but unwilling to make a scene in front of the other students. By the time we entered the building, my legs ached. He pointed me in the direction of my room.

"I'll be here when you get out and take you to your next class."

I shot him a look of irritation but didn't have time to argue, already late for class. The only empty desk stood at the back of the room. I unobtrusively took my seat and laced my fingers together on top of my books, waiting as roll was called.

My first class was freshman English, my favorite subject. Still, I was nervous, afraid I wouldn't be able to keep up with the older students. The instructor looked to be in his mid-thirties. His long hair curled at the base of his neck. He was clean-shaven and wore a suit coat which he immediately took off. He loosened his tie and rolled up his shirtsleeves.

He wrote a sentence across the long blackboard and held up the chalk. "Who can diagram this sentence?"

We had diagrammed harder sentences in Miss Weaver's class. When no one else volunteered, I timidly raised my hand.

He pointed to me. "Miss . . .?"

I climbed to my feet. "Sarah Jane Hunter, sir."

He handed me the chalk, and I walked to the board. I wiped the sweat from my hands and went to work. When I finished, he nodded his head with approval.

"Good job, Miss Hunter."

I returned to my seat.

Maybe college would be easier than I thought.

Michael waited for me as he had promised. His eyes lit up when he saw me, and my heart again was disloyal, skipping a beat.

He pulled out my map from his pocket. "Okay, follow me, and I'll show you your next class."

I shook my head. "I think I can figure it out now. Thanks for your help."

He studied me for a moment and handed the paper to me. "I didn't tell her, Jay."

I searched his eyes, oblivious to the people swarming around us, wanting desperately to believe him. What did it matter anyway? From what I heard, he was still dating Sylvia. And I still dated Daniel. And I still smelled Michael's "cologne." From the look of his rumpled clothes and unshaven face, he was still drinking.

I sighed. "It doesn't matter anymore, does it? Bye, Michael." I walked away, my head down. When I glanced back over my shoulder, he was gone.

I found my next class, after only five minutes of searching. The teacher droned on and on about what was expected of us. But, all I could see, all I could think of was Michael, the way he had looked, what he had said.

The class was over, and half the class already filtered into the hall before I knew it. I gathered my things and made a beeline for the door. Luckily, I had a two-hour break before my next class.

I wandered around and found a park-like area with benches under the trees. I opened my lunch bag that Aunt Liza had made from scraps of material. While better than the old syrup bucket, it still held the same ingredients— biscuits and figs with a piece of sausage. I ate my lunch and opened up my books, planning to get a head start on my homework.

But I couldn't concentrate. Why couldn't I get Michael out of my mind? I sighed. No way would I have a B average at this rate. My only hope was to completely avoid Michael, fleeing if I saw him before he saw me. His nearness addled me, as Momma would say.

Clothed In Thunder

I grabbed my things and decided to find my next class. It was a good thing I decided to when I did. Even with my map, I got lost several times and had to ask directions twice. Students already entered when I arrived. When I glanced around, I almost stamped my feet in frustration.

Michael was just ahead of me. Just great and gravy.

I pretended not to see him and found a seat as far away from him as possible. If I had found it difficult to concentrate before; now it was impossible. My eyes were continually drawn to him. It was easy for Marla to say just ignore him. She wasn't me.

Something would have to give. I sighed heavily and strove to tame my unruly thoughts.

No, at this rate, I would never get over him.

And that was unfair to Daniel.

And to me.

Chapter 26--Uncle Howard

When I arrived home, I was hot and sweaty. I got a wash pan and cool water, sponged off and changed my clothes. Aunt Liza fixed us a glass of iced tea, and we sat on the front porch, using square cardboard fans from church to help keep us cool.

"How did today go?" she asked.

"Fine." I pushed back a strand of damp hair.

"Fine? Tell me all about it." She took a sip of her iced tea.

"Michael was there. He's in one of my classes." I rolled the tea glass across my hot forehead.

"I wonder why he's in a freshman class. That seems strange."

It did seem strange now that she mentioned it. Did he make a note of my class and sneak in just to be near me? Part of me flushed with excitement at the thought. Part of me was annoyed. I groaned and covered my face with my fan.

"Jay, are you okay?"

I waved a hand. "Fine. It's just hard."

She leaned forward, her unique vanilla scent surrounding me. She pushed my fan away from my face. "Are your classes too hard?"

"No, my classes are fine. I meant life is hard. I can't get over Michael, no matter how hard I try. . ."

"Sweetie, you need to resolve this." She surveyed me solemnly.

We remained silent for a few minutes.

I made an effort to lower my hands to my lap. Chance came to me and laid his head on my knee. I rubbed him, and he whimpered softly. "Maybe it was a mistake to come back. I should have moved in with Momma. Stayed as far away from Michael as I could."

Aunt Liza shook her head vehemently. "Don't say that, Jay! Look at what opportunities have opened for you. You're only sixteen, and you're in college with a scholarship. You will be one of the first women veterinarians to graduate. I think you're where you need to be."

"But Michael is making me miserable. . ."

"You're letting him make you miserable. There's a difference."

"But I don't know how to forget him. I've tried. . ." My voice broke. I twisted away and blinked back tears.

"All this stress is hard on you. It'll get better. Wait and see."

"I hope so, but I don't see how."

She patted my back. "Why don't you go write Dan a letter? Or, go for a ride? Just put Michael out of your mind."

"I'll write Daniel when I finish my homework. I've got a ton of it." I rose and planted a kiss on her forehead before going in.

When I finished my homework, I did write Daniel a long letter, longer than I planned. I told him I felt overwhelmed but decided not to go into details about Michael.

In a few days I received a letter in response. Daniel said it was such a warm September that we could take a trip to the beach. He was sure it would cheer me up.

I'd never been to the beach, and it seemed like a perfect getaway. Daniel urged me to invite Marla, Andrew, Anne, and Tommy.

Aunt Liza gave me permission but only if the others were going with us.

Clothed In Thunder

I walked over to Marla's with Chance. The sun bore down, the thick canopy of leaves doing little to cool me from the oppressive heat.

Marla sat on a bench under a large oak tree with Grace. Marla seemed so serene with her head bent slightly down, checking Grace's homework. The tilt of her head reminded me of a painting we had seen at school of a French mother washing her child. Marla and Grace were a living imitation of the painting.

When Grace finally took her homework and went in to wash up for supper, I moved closer to Marla. "I came over to ask you a question."

Marla turned her full attention to me. "Yes?"

"Do you think your parents would let you go to the beach with us—Daniel and me?" I watched her anxiously, wondering if she thought it would be a good idea.

"It sounds like fun. I'll ask tonight and let you know."

"Okay. And, can you see if the others want to go, too?"

"Andrew's coming over later. I'm sure he'll want to go, and he can ask Ann and Tommy, too.

"Great! I'll see you tomorrow then." I whistled for Chance.

He stayed on my heels all the way home. I walked to the barn to tend the horses before heading back to the house. Chance ran ahead of me, barking at squirrels and chasing them up the trees.

As I neared the back porch, Uncle Howard came out of the house, holding a bottle in his hand.

"Hi, Uncle Howard."

He startled and hid the bottle behind his back. "Oh, hi, Jay." He stepped backwards toward his shop. "Just going to my shop," he mumbled.

I caught my breath. *Michael had meant Uncle Howard.* The bottle was evidence, wasn't it? Sadness draped over me. Somehow, I would have to get Uncle Howard help.

I'd ask Daniel--maybe he'd know what to do.

I went into the house and looked around the kitchen, disoriented for a moment. Then I knew why. Aunt Liza had not started supper. I went to look for her. She was in the bedroom with the curtains pulled. One arm hid her eyes.

"Aunt Liza? Are you okay?"

She raised herself on one elbow. "No, I have a sick headache. Jay, can you make supper for you and Howard?"

"Yes, ma'am. Is there anything you need?"

"No, child. If I can get some sleep, I'll feel better tomorrow."

"Call me if you need me."

"I will." She rolled away from me.

I quietly closed the door and tiptoed to the kitchen. As I prepared supper, I reflected. If she had found out about Uncle Howard, that might be why she had a migraine.

I shook my head. Men! They were all alike.

When I had finished supper, I called Uncle Howard in from his shop. But I didn't eat with him. I carried my plate to my room, using my homework as an excuse.

Marla came over the next afternoon, her eyes bright. "Momma and Poppa told me I could go. I've already talked to Andrew and Anne, and they have permission also."

I was in the swing on the front porch, and I let my feet scrape against the floorboards.

"You don't look too happy." Marla sat down in a chair beside the swing.

I didn't want to tell her about Uncle Howard. I cast around for something else. "Um . . . I don't have a bathing suit and no money to buy one."

"I believe my mother has an old one. I think it will fit you."

"Really? You don't think she would mind if I borrowed it?"

"She'll probably give it to you. I don't think it fits her anymore."

I smiled my thanks. "Good. I'll write Daniel and tell him we all want to go."

Uncle Howard opened the front door and stuck his head out. "Jay. . .Oh, sorry, I didn't know you had company." He opened the door wider and stepped out. "Hello, Miss Phillips. How're you doing today?"

"Fine."

"Fine as frog hair split three ways," I said listlessly.

"What did you say?" Marla asked.

"Oh, nothing. It's just something my poppa used to say." And Michael. Hadn't he once said that? A pang pierced me. If only Poppa were here, he could help me deal with Uncle Howard and Michael, tell me what I should do.

Uncle Howard beamed at us. "Ladies, I've got a job. I've got to go get some measurements. I wanted to let Jay know where I'd be."

"What kind of job?" I asked.

"I'll be making a few chairs, a table, and a couple of other things. Maybe this time it'll work out. Keep your fingers crossed." He disappeared back into the house.

"I've got to get going, too. Night!" Marla bounded down the steps.

I only had time enough to call "good night" before she disappeared. I rose and stretched, then went inside to begin my homework, praying that Uncle Howard would be able to do this job without drinking.

Chapter 27--Beach Trip

Daniel picked me up early on Saturday morning. We drove to Marla's house where Marla and Andrew were already waiting on the front steps.

"Hi," I said. "Where's Anne and Tommy?"

They didn't answer, just exchanged a look, before climbing into the backseat.

It wasn't until Daniel pulled into the street that Marla spoke. "They're going to ride with Michael and Sylvia."

"Michael and Sylvia?" My mouth fell open, and I twisted in my seat to get a better look at her face.

Marla shot me a look of apology. "Andrew was talking to Sylvia and let the cat out of the bag."

We both frowned at Andrew.

He shrugged. "She kinda invited herself. It's a free country. I can't stop them from going. What's the big deal anyway?" He ground his teeth, his eyes angry.

Marla had probably been chewing him out. "It's not a big deal. The more, the merrier," I said bitterly.

Marla whispered to him in the back, and Andrew raised a voice in protest followed by an "Ouch." Marla probably punched him.

"Really, Marla, it's not a problem." I set my face in a determined smile. I'd have fun no matter who was there.

But wasn't the whole idea of the trip to help me forget about Michael? Somehow, I'd just have to stay as far away from him as possible.

We arrived at the beach, and there was no sign of the others. Maybe they had changed their minds.

Marla and I wore our bathing suits under our dresses. Daniel and Andrew walked down to the beach while Marla and I stayed in the car to peel our dresses off. Literally, we had to peel. The high humidity had our dresses sticking to us.

Clothed In Thunder

Marla wore sandals, but I didn't have a pair. I took my shoes off and left them in the car before we followed Daniel and Andrew down to the beach.

Daniel let out a low whistle when he saw us. "You girls look beautiful."

His eyes swept over both of us but lingered a moment longer on Marla. She wore a blue bathing suit that matched her eyes. The sun reflected off her golden curls.

I, on the other hand, wore an old-fashioned black suit. The neckline was high and the bottom of the suit covered half my thighs. I'm sure when the suit had been new, Marla's mom had worn black stockings with it. My legs and feet were bare.

No other people were on the beach. Probably September was late in the year for most beach goers. We spread our blankets out, and Marla and I stretched out on one of them.

Both Andrew and Daniel wore dark trunks and dark tank tops. They removed the tank tops before splashing into the water.

Marla's gaze followed Daniel. "Wow. He's so muscular. He looks really strong," she whispered to me.

"That's what the army will do for you."

Marla laughed. "I'll see if I can get Andrew to join when we graduate."

I nodded, casting around for something nice to say about Andrew. He looked puny next to Daniel. I decided not to say anything.

I laid back and closed my eyes. The sun bore down relentlessly. It reminded me of the story Poppa told Zeke and me.

The Indians had loved the sun so much they asked God to let it shine all the time. God did, and the plants grew in profusion making it difficult to even walk. The people could not sleep.

I must have, though. I dreamed the vines intertwined about me, cutting off my breath.

Marla poked me in the ribs, and I sat up.

"They're here," she whispered.

"Hey," Anne called.

Marla and I stood up, brushing the sand away.

Anne looked cross, and even Tommy's normally good-natured face had a frown, although he lit up when he saw us.

"You girls look great."

Marla blushed, and I felt my own cheeks grow warm.

Anne had on a modest suit, similar to Marla's. She and Tommy continued on to the water's edge.

Sylvia approached with Michael trailing behind her. She had a thin covering over her suit, some kind of garment I'd never seen before that clung to her curves.

"Hi, girls," she said, the edge of her lips barely lifting.

"Hi, Sylvia, Michael," Marla said. "Did you have any trouble finding us?"

"No," Michael said, smiling. "We saw Daniel's car and knew we were at the right place."

"He has a gorgeous car," Sylvia said. This time her lips made it into a smile. She turned to Michael. "Going in?"

She reached to the hem of the covering and skimmed it over her head.

Marla gasped, and I think I did, too. Sylvia's suit, in two pieces, bared her midriff. Her suit revealed almost her entire leg. The material clung to every curve, just as the covering had, and the top dipped low.

I threw Michael a covert glance to see his reaction. His forehead was furrowed, whether from the glare of the sun or another emotion, I didn't know. Without speaking, he sprinted the short distance and dove into the water.

Sylvia followed to the water's edge at a leisurely pace. The waves broke at her feet. She motioned to Michael, and he came to her. I don't think she was expecting his reaction. He grasped her elbow and escorted her down the beach. Sylvia's voice, shrill above the pounding waves, reached to us. I heard, "What do you think you are doing?" and "Let go of me."

I felt like we were eavesdropping. "Come on, Marla." I rushed down the sloped sand and into the waves. Anne and the boys met us, splashing and chasing us through the waves. Daniel caught me in his arms.

"Let's swim out farther," he whispered in my ear.

"What? I don't want to go out farther." This was my first trip to the ocean. I felt safe here near the shore. I didn't want to get away from its safety.

"There's a section where the water isn't over our heads. We can swim out to a place where the waves are not breaking." He pointed. "See? The water won't be as deep there."

"Okay. I'll see if the others want to swim that far out."

He reached out a hand as if to stop me but let it drop back on the water. I splashed over to Marla and Anne.

"Daniel and I are going to swim out farther. Do y'all want to?"

"Are you crazy, Jay?" Tommy said. "I'm not going out any deeper than my waist."

"Daniel says the water's not as deep a little farther out." I pointed to the spot.

Both girls shook their heads. Tommy and Andrew also refused to go.

I made my way back to Daniel. "They don't want to go."

"Good. Just you and me then."

"I don't want to go."

"You just said you would."

"I meant with the others."

"You don't trust me, Jay?"

I let my eyes drift around us. Michael had left Sylvia on the shore and splashed in our direction. I turned back to meet Daniel's eyes. "I trust you. Let's go."

Daniel led the way, grasping my hand. When the water reached my chin, I dove, following in Daniel's wake, swimming beneath the waves. The salt water burned my eyes and all was blurry, but I managed to keep him in sight.

When he stopped in front of me, my feet sought to find a solid surface but only found water. Daniel caught me and pulled me close to him.

He laughed. "I'm sorry. I forgot you were shorter. Let's move a little farther out. I don't think it's as deep right over there."

He towed me a short distance until I was able to feel the sand beneath me. My chin touched the water's surface.

I looked back toward the shore and saw we weren't as far out as I thought. The emerald green water lapped around us gently instead of crashing over us as the waves did closer to the shore.

"It is nice out here," I said.

A few white feathery clouds edged the blue sky. Birds spread their wings overhead.

He smiled and raised an eyebrow. "It sure is."

Then, he dove under the water. He popped back up with a shell in his hand. "Check this out." He handed me the shell.

"Wow. That's beautiful." I flipped it in my hands, admiring the perfect swirls.

"I'll see if I can find any more." He dove back under.

I spotted Sylvia again, still walking along the edge of the water, but now with Andrew beside her.

How did Marla feel about that? Marla and Anne were sitting on the blanket. Tommy was still in the water, the waves crashing over him, sometimes knocking him off his feet. I didn't see Michael anywhere.

Daniel resurfaced. "Two more."

"Nice. Do you know what I'd like to do?"

A smile played around his lips as he shook his head.

"I want to float on my back, but I'm afraid I'll float away."

"I'll hold you. You can trust me."

I nodded. "I know." I let myself fall back into the water, my legs rising. I bobbed like a cork.

Daniel's hand closed around my left wrist. "I've got you. You can float all you want."

"Thanks." I watched the sea birds flying overhead. Their calling and the sound of the waves soothed me. All my tension melted away. I wished I could sleep like this, supported by the waves, held by Daniel. Like floating on the cream instead of endlessly swimming. The waves gently bobbed me up and down.

And then Daniel's hand slipped from my wrist, and I drifted away.

Chapter 28--The Ocean

J floundered for a moment, my head ducking beneath the waves. I came up coughing and sputtering. Daniel grabbed my arm and pulled me until I found my footing again. I raked my hair out of my eyes, and Michael gazed at me solemnly, his eyes slightly unfocused.

"Sorry. I didn't mean to bump into y'all. Can't see a thing in this salty water."

"It's blurry, but you can see shapes," Daniel said, his face thunderous.

Michael shook his head. "Maybe you can see better than I can."

Daniel moved closer to Michael. "Maybe you need to open your eyes!"

I placed a hand on Daniel's arm, afraid of his anger. "Daniel, I'm sure Michael didn't mean to bump you." But I wasn't sure if I told the truth. Maybe Michael *had* bumped into Daniel on purpose.

Daniel glared at Michael, his muscles tense. Michael returned his look with a hint of defiance.

Suddenly, I felt drained. "I'm swimming back." I didn't wait for a reply but dove into the water. I swam underneath until the water became too shallow to swim in. I stood, the waves crashing into me, knocking me to my knees. I clambered back up and scurried out of the water before it had a chance to knock me down again.

I made it up the incline and dropped to the blanket beside Marla. Tommy and Anne were on the other blanket next to us. Andrew and Sylvia still walked along the beach.

Marla handed me a towel, and I dried off. I wrapped the towel around my shoulders and tried not to look, but my eyes were drawn to the spot where I had left Michael and Daniel.

Neither was there. My eyes swept the area. Neither one was in sight.

"Marla, where are Michael and Daniel?" I tried to keep my voice calm.

She pointed, and I saw a dark shape under the water, swimming farther out. I couldn't tell if it was Michael or Daniel.

"I only see one. Where's the other one?" My voice rose.

Tommy propped on his elbows. "What's wrong?"

I pointed. "Michael and Daniel. I only see one of them."

Marla draped an arm over my shoulder. "I'm sure they're okay. They're both strong swimmers."

Anne came and knelt beside me. She shaded her eyes with one hand. "That dark shape under the water? Are you sure that's a person? It looks like a shark."

My heart pounded in my chest. I had never even considered sharks the whole time I was in the ocean. I shaded my eyes as Anne had done.

"That's a person." *It had to be.* But it was only one shape. Where was the other one? I felt sick to my stomach. If anything happened, it would be my fault.

Tommy climbed to his feet. "There's someone else. Over there." He pointed to the left.

A head bobbed above the water. *Definitely a person.*

Sylvia and Andrew sauntered over to us.

"What are you looking at?" Andrew asked.

I looked at him, slightly disgusted. Why had he left Marla to go traipsing after Sylvia?

"Michael or Daniel. They're too far out for us to tell." I clenched my hands into fists.

Sylvia yawned and dropped to the blanket. "I think I'll take a nap."

I ignored her, too worried to care what she did. "What are we going to do?" My nails cut into my palms.

Marla patted my arm. "I'm sure they'll be all right." But I heard the doubt in her voice.

There was nothing I could do. Lifeguards did not patrol this beach.

Both dark figures continued farther and farther from the shore. Were they caught in an undercurrent? I chewed my bottom lip. *I couldn't stay here and watch this.*

I scrambled up.

"Where are you going?" Marla asked.

"I don't know. Maybe I can find help." I started to slough through the sand.

"Anne and I will go with you," Marla said.

"Sure," Anne said.

We walked away from the water. I tried not to look back but couldn't help but turn once. I no longer saw them. *Only the ocean spreading to the horizon.*

What were they thinking? Did they fight over me and get swept out? Surely, neither would be that stupid. But what happened?

We might never know. Helplessness washed over me.

I gulped deep breaths. I kept going until I reached Daniel's car. *There were no other cars in the area.* Should I drive for help?

A gnarled tree nearby offered the only shade. I sat down cross-legged on the ground and tried to think. Anne and Marla knelt beside me. Without asking, Marla took my hand and Anne's and began to pray.

I reached for Anne's hand and bowed my head, too. My thoughts raced, and I could barely focus on what Marla said. *God. Help. Give us peace.*

And, amazingly, I did feel more peaceful.

"Thank you, Marla," I said.

"I'm sure they'll be okay," Anne said.

Marla reached a hand to rub my arm. "Do you want to go back and see if they've returned?"

"Should we go find someone to help?" I asked, doubtfully.

"How? Do you have Daniel's keys?" Anne asked.

I had not even thought to get the keys. "I guess we've got to go back and look for the keys, if they're not back. . ." I arose on shaky legs.

Marla took my arm. "I'm sure they will be."

We made our way back, and I prayed with each step that they had returned. My pulse thumped loudly in my ears as we neared. Tommie and Andrew were at the water's edge, helping someone stand.

It was Daniel.

"Is he okay?" I called, running to them.

Daniel smiled and managed a wink. "Fine. Just tired."

The boys helped him to the blanket, and he laid back, his eyes closed. I knelt beside him. "Are you okay?" I repeated.

"Fine. Just need to catch my breath."

I touched his arm, and he opened his eyes.

"Where's Michael? Is he okay?" I asked.

Daniel frowned at me. "Fine." He took a shuddering breath. "On a sand bar."

My heart steadied, and I breathed a sigh of relief. "What happened?"

"Let me catch my breath." He closed his eyes, and I backed away.

Marla and Anne had both hovered behind me and heard Daniel. Marla squeezed my shoulder but didn't say anything. I could read the relief on both their faces.

But Michael wasn't out of the woods. A troubling thought crossed my mind. What if Daniel lied? What if Michael had drowned and Dan was just afraid to tell me? Afraid because it had been his fault? Surely, he didn't harm Michael. Did he? But he could have hurt him without really meaning to.

I chewed my bottom lip, sitting back on my heels. No, he would never hurt Michael. I trusted Daniel. He had changed. He was not the Dan Drake who hurt others. Hadn't I just told him I trusted him?

Andrew shouted, and my eyes swept over the area he pointed to. A tiny dot drew slowly closer.

Daniel rose on his elbows. "Is it Michael?"

"I think so," I said.

"Good." He flopped back down. "Tell him I win."

Win? *They had some kind of bet?* Anger surged through me.

Stupid boys. Scaring me like this. Scaring everyone.

When the others, except for Daniel and Sylvia, ran to meet Michael, I stayed seated on the blanket, gritting my teeth.

Neither Daniel nor Sylvia bothered sitting up. Sylvia's floppy straw hat covered her face and not a muscle moved. I didn't know if she slept or just pretended.

Michael came out of the water on his own volition. His eyes sparkled in the sun, and he smiled up toward us. I tried to avert my gaze, but my eyes continually drew back to him as he made his way up the incline.

Marla ran ahead of him and spread out another blanket. He dropped down with a smooth motion.

"That was fun," he said. He tilted his head and glanced up at the four who had gathered around him.

"Fun?" Marla said angrily. "You had us worried to death, especially Jay!"

Michael looked contrite. "Sorry. I just didn't think. I saw the dolphins and followed them."

"You saw dolphins?" Andrew asked, his face lighting up.

"Yeah. Dan didn't tell you?"

Several heads shook.

I pulled my gaze away and stared out at the ocean, clenching my teeth, angrier than I had been in a very long time.

Chapter 29--A Hoot

Michael grinned. "Five. There were five dolphins."

I glared at him. "Daniel said to tell you that he wins. I hope y'all had fun."

"Yeah." He grinned at me. "I thought there were only four. He said five."

Marla's brows drew together, and she placed her hands on her hips, looking like a teacher. "And y'all swam after them just to prove who was right?"

"No." Michael grinned. "I had an opportunity to swim with dolphins. I wasn't going to pass that up." He flashed a smile. "That was something."

Daniel propped on his elbows and looked up at our faces. "I did it to win."

"What?" *Was he crazy? Worrying me just to win some stupid bet?* "Do you always have to win?"

He gave me a funny look. "Yep. Always."

"I wish I had been with you," Tommy said.

Anne laughed. "Tommy, I believe you said you weren't going any farther than waist-deep? Or, was it knee-deep?"

"Yeah, but if I had known there were dolphins . . . "

Anne shook her head and laughed at him.

Michael glanced at me. "Daniel turned around to come back, refusing to rest with me. He was afraid Jay would be worried."

Daniel pushed into a sitting position. "Don't be telling her that!"

I shifted away from him. "Don't ever do that again!"

"I'm sorry, Jay. We didn't mean to worry you." Daniel didn't look sorry. I was sure he'd do it all again if he had the chance.

Here I had imagined them fighting over me. Instead, they swam after dolphins. I drew my knees to my chin and wrapped my arms around my legs.

Everyone started talking and laughing at once, even Sylvia who had finally removed her hat and was sitting up.

After a few minutes, Anne stood. "I'm turning into a lobster. I've got to get out of the sun, or I'll be burnt to a crisp."

"It's about time to go anyway," Marla said.

"Awwww, 'Momma'," Andrew said in a whiny voice. "Do we have to?"

But everyone got up and began gathering the blankets and towels, shaking out as much of the sand as possible.

"I know a restaurant that's not too expensive," Daniel said. "We can stop there on the way back." Everyone nodded agreement while Daniel explained where it was located.

When we got to the cars, Sylvia looked at Daniel's car longingly. "I wish I could ride with y'all." She poked out her bottom lip in a pout.

Michael studied her for a moment before turning to Marla and Andrew. "Do y'all want to switch with us?"

I pulled Daniel aside. "Tell him no," I whispered.

He shook his head and made a motion of bringing a drink to his lips.

"He's drinking?" I hissed.

"Both of them."

"Both?" I hadn't bothered lowering my voice. How did he know? Did Michael tell him?

"Who's going to drive your truck?" Andrew was asking.

"Well, that's between you and Tommy. Unless one of the girls wants to drive." He held the key up in the air, and both boys grabbed for it.

They play-tussled before Marla broke them up. "You can take turns."

Tommy swirled to face her. "But who gets to drive first?"

"Anyone have a quarter?" Anne asked.

Daniel rummaged in his car. "Will a dime do?"

Marla took charge of the dime and flipped it. Andrew called out heads. Marla caught it and slapped it on the back of her hand. Both boys crowded around as she slowly lifted her hand.

"Tails!" Tommy shouted. He danced around, snatching the keys from Michael's hand. He grabbed Anne's hand. "Let's go."

Michael held out his arm as if he changed his mind and then dropped it. He shrugged his shoulders. "Marla will keep him straight."

"Hopefully," I said.

Michael and Sylvia laughed as we climbed into Daniel's car.

Sylvia leaned forward and shook a finger at Daniel. "I knew Michael would do something crazy like swimming after dolphins, but I thought you had more sense, Dan."

When Daniel didn't answer, Sylvia moved back, and I heard kissing sounds. I thought Michael was mad with her for wearing that immodest suit. He sure got over that in a hurry—if he had been mad at all. I didn't understand him. Drunk or not, what did he think he was doing?

But who cared what Sylvia and Michael did? I moved closer to Daniel, and he took my hand.

"Hey, Jay," Michael said. "How're you liking biology? Professor Paxton's a hoot, isn't he?"

I twisted around and stared at Michael. "A hoot?" The Michael I knew didn't talk like that.

Michael leaned forward, his breath warm on my neck, and I caught a whiff of the alcohol.

Daniel had been right. But had I really doubted him?

"Professor Paxton clutches his stomach with one hand while he writes notes on the blackboard," Michael said.

"Why does he do that?" Sylvia asked.

"He's been teaching about parasites. We all think he's a hypochondriac, imagining all those worms wiggling inside him."

I forced myself to laugh along with Michael.

Yeah, Professor Paxton was a hoot.

We pulled into the graveled parking lot. Well, once it had been graveled but now dirt covered most of it. Weeds poked up everywhere. A couple of other cars were parked out front along with Michael's truck.

Tommy had beaten us there. The four of them waited for us at the door.

"How long have you been here?" I asked.

"Ten minutes or so," Anne said. "It would have been longer if Marla and I hadn't screamed at Tommy to slow down. I think he was going eighty-five at one point."

Tommy cleared his throat. "Ninety, actually." His ears reddened more than they already were, and he ducked his head.

"Ninety?" Michael said. "Wow, Tommy. I didn't think the old truck would go that fast."

"It was shaking sugar in the gourd," Andrew said.

"It felt like it was about to fly apart." Anne pushed the hair away from her face. "I'm still shaking!"

"Oh, you loved it." Andrew punched his sister's arm.

"Ouch! I'm burnt. Don't touch me!"

Anne's face was red, along with every other part of her body that showed. Andrew, too. The others had varying degrees of redness.

Marla put a hand to her face. "Am I as red as Anne?"

"No," Daniel said. "You look great." His eyes brightened as he surveyed her.

What was going on? Was he trying to make me jealous? I had to admit Marla did look exceptionally pretty with her cheeks rosy and her golden hair windblown around her face. I probably looked a mess. I pulled my hair back from my face and tried to smooth it as we entered the restaurant. The waitress led us to a table.

Tommy glanced around when we were seated. "Yep, looks like everyone is burnt. Everyone except Jay."

Sylvia studied me for a moment. "I wonder why she didn't burn." She spoke as if I were not even present.

I caught her eye and spoke a little louder than normal. "My skin's darker because my grandmother was an Indian. I usually don't burn."

"Oh, how interesting," Sylvia said. She turned to Michael. "Do many Indians live near your home?"

I rolled my eyes, and Marla frowned at Sylvia.

Michael grinned at me. "Jay's the only wild one."

Sylvia laughed, and I seethed.

Tilting my chin back, I glared at Michael. "I'm proud of my heritage. What's wrong with having Indian blood?"

"Nothing!" Michael held his hands in the air as if in surrender. "Nothing at all."

Daniel draped his arm over the back of my chair as the waitress arrived to take our order. He squeezed my shoulder. I don't know if he was warning me that it was no use arguing with a drunk person.

Clothed In Thunder

I didn't speak to Michael or Sylvia for the rest of the meal. Or on the rest of the way home either.

When Daniel dropped me off, he told me he was on furlough and planned to go back home for a couple of days before coming back to see me.

Chapter 30--The Argument

Aunt Liza was waiting up when I went into the house.

"Did you have a good time?" Her forehead was furrowed, her eyes red, and I wondered if she had another migraine.

I considered her question. Parts were fun. But, most of it had not been. I dropped down beside her on the couch and told her about my day, leaving out the drinking part.

When I told her about the dolphins, she laughed until tears rolled down her cheeks.

"I didn't think it was funny, Aunt Liza."

She gazed at me with her turquoise eyes and smiled. "One day you'll think so. One day you'll look back on this with fond memories."

I looked down at my hands, shaking my head. I couldn't imagine this day ever being funny. "Let me tell you what happened when we stopped to eat. Sylvia wanted to know why I didn't burn, and I told her it was probably because of my Indian blood. Sylvia asked Michael if any Indians lived nearby, and he said 'Jay's the only wild one.'"

Aunt Liza chuckled. "Well, child, wasn't any harm in that. He was just teasing you."

I was tired and got up, yawning. "Where's Uncle Howard?"

"He's gone to bed. Wasn't feeling well." She stood and stretched. "And speaking of bed, it's about my bedtime."

"I think I'll go to bed too. Got up early this morning. My day's been exhausting."

She kissed my forehead. "Good night. Sleep tight."

"You, too."

I went to my bedroom and got ready for bed. But once I turned off the light and lay down on the bed, I couldn't sleep.

I kept replaying the events of the day. Michael, no telling how much he had been drinking, swimming out so far. He could have died.

When Daniel dropped me off, he had assured me he would make sure Michael got back to the dorm in one piece. Angry as I was, I felt better knowing Daniel was taking care of Michael. Both of them had acted foolishly today. *And, Sylvia!* Flirting with Andrew, wearing that skimpy bathing suit.

I don't know how long my thoughts tumbled when I heard the voices.

I raised up on my elbows and listened. Was that Uncle Howard? His voice thundered through the small house. Aunt Liza had said he wasn't feeling well, but he didn't sound sick now. Was he drunk?

I couldn't make sense of his words. I strained to understand, but his voice dropped, and all I heard was murmuring.

I had never heard them argue before. True, Uncle Howard appeared angry that day I arrived home without Zeke, but I never learned about what.

The voices faded away, and I rolled over and into sleep.

The next morning, I stumbled to the kitchen, yawning. Aunt Liza, still in her gown, sat at the kitchen table drinking coffee.

The clock on the mantle couldn't be right. "What time is it?" I asked.

"It's eleven o'clock." She took a sip of her coffee without looking at me.

"We're going to miss church!"

She waved toward a chair, motioning me to sit down. "We're not going today."

"Why? Is something wrong with Uncle Howard?"

I noticed for the first time her red-rimmed eyes. "Aunt Liza, what's wrong?"

"Howard lost the job."

"Again?" I fell into the chair.

She took my hand in hers. "And that's not all. He's gone."

"Gone?" Fear clutched my heart. "Gone where?"

She shook her head and bit her bottom lip.

"Aunt Liza, where is he?"

"I don't know. He was gone when I got up this morning." She lowered her forehead into her hands.

"Surely he's around somewhere. He wouldn't just leave."

She raised her head. "His clothes are gone. His watch, his billfold." She shrugged her shoulders. "I've looked everywhere. He's not here."

"Maybe he's just out looking for work."

"He would have told me." She glanced into her coffee cup. "Besides, it's Sunday. Nothing's open today."

"Do you want to go to the police?"

"No."

"Get someone. The preacher? The neighbors?"

"No, Jay. This is between Howard and me. I don't want to drag anyone else into it." She pushed her chair back. "I'm going to lie down for a while."

I put a hand out to stop her. "Is there anything I can do? Do you want any breakfast?" I searched her eyes.

She blanched. "No, no. I just need some quiet. I have a bad headache."

"Call me if you need anything."

"I will, dear."

She left. I, too, felt sick to my stomach. I got up and poured a cup of coffee but couldn't drink it. I threw it out the back door. I decided I would go ahead and get dressed.

It was so hot in the kitchen that I didn't wait for the water to heat much. I took a lukewarm bath and washed my hair.

After I emptied out the water, I went back to my room to comb out my hair and to dress.

At a loss. I paced the floor, my stomach churning. Only silence came from Aunt Liza's room.

Had she checked the shop to make sure Uncle Howard wasn't there, sleeping on one of the cots? Maybe in an alcoholic stupor like Michael had been when he had slept in his truck? I decided to go check.

I went out the back and pushed open the door to his shop.

I clicked on the light. The mess startled me. Tools lay strewn across the shelves and pieces of wood, still with nails sticking through them, littered the floor.

This mess looked like Uncle Howard had made something, smashed it to pieces, and thrown his tools down. Maybe he had gotten angry about losing his job and done this. I sat on the stool and looked around.

Uncle Howard, so gentle and soft-spoken. This just didn't seem like him. Is this what drinking led to?

In the corner, beneath the cradle, the wooden boxes threatened to topple over. An old cloth draped over them, hiding the contents. I walked over and pulled the cloth off. Gin bottles had been thrown into the boxes.

Empty gin bottles.

I walked to Aunt Liza's room, not sure if I was doing the right thing. I knocked on the door, hiding the bottle behind my back.

"Come in." Aunt Liza's voice was hoarse.

I turned the knob and stepped over the threshold.

Chapter 31--Finding Michael

Aunt Liza lay on the bed, a washrag covering her eyes. She lifted a corner to gaze at me before letting it fall back in place. I approached the bed.

"Aunt Liza, I found something . . . I don't know if you knew about this . . ."

"What, child?" She rose on one elbow, letting the rag fall to the bed.

I held out the gin bottle. She pulled herself up with a visible effort. She let her legs dangle from the bed as her eyes widened.

"Where did you get that?" She reached out to take it from my hand.

"Uncle Howard's shop. In a box."

She stared at the bottle in her hand, her eyes unfocused, not speaking.

Did she not understand Uncle Howard had been drinking? And from the number of bottles, had been drinking a long time? Hadn't she smelled the gin on him?

"Aunt Liza," I said gently. "Don't you think Uncle Howard is drinking?"

She looked at me, startled. "Drinking? Howard?" She laughed a sad laugh.

"Yes. This isn't the only bottle. The whole corner is filled." I sat down next to her.

"The corner?" Her face drooped along with her shoulders.

"Yes, he's been drinking a long time."

She shook her head. "No. Howard doesn't drink."

"Aunt Liza! All of these bottles? How do you explain that?" I slumped down.

She raked her fingers through her hair. "I. . .Maybe he found them?" She shrugged her shoulders.

"Okay. I just thought you should know." I sighed. Why wouldn't she believe me?

"Jay, will you just take it back? Put it back where you found it. Just leave me be? Please?"

She just wasn't ready to face facts.

"If you don't need anything. . ."

She picked up the rag and held it to her eyes. "No. Go." She shooed me away with a wave of her hand.

I sighed and left her.

I had to find Uncle Howard, convince him to get help. But how? Where could I find someone to help me?

It was another sweltering day. I tried to imagine where Uncle Howard would have gone. To the church building? It might be one place to start looking. Services were over. Everyone would have left by now, except, maybe the preacher. I could ask him what to do.

I entered into the coolness of the church. The high-ceilinged building with windows on each side, rising almost the full height of the wall, caught the slightest of breezes. Large oak trees surrounded the outside, keeping it shaded.

A person knelt at the second pew. His hands lay on the back of the pew in front of him, and his head rested against them.

I recognized him immediately. *Michael.* Why was he here in Plainsville instead of at Auburn?

"What are you doing here?" I exclaimed before I could stop myself.

He turned his head and looked at me with his liquid brown eyes, rimmed in red.

"Is there anything wrong?" I asked.

He didn't move from where he knelt, didn't seem embarrassed, just smiled up at me. "Of course nothing's wrong. Just enjoying the quiet."

Clothed In Thunder

"I didn't know you attended church here." I knew he didn't. I'd never seen him at services before.

"I don't. I don't go to church anywhere. I was just, um. . .looking for a cool place. What are you doing here?" He finally rose from his knees and seated himself.

I slid into the pew beside him, twisting my hands together in my lap. "Uncle Howard is missing."

"Missing? What do you mean?"

"He's gone. We don't know where he's at."

"Did you go to the police?"

I shook my head. "No. He took a suitcase with him. He left on his own."

"Oh."

"Do you think . . . Will you help me look for him?"

"I don't know, Jay." He studied me for a second. "Maybe he doesn't want to be found."

"But I've got to find him. For Aunt Liza."

"Jay, does she want you to find him? Did she send you out to look for him?"

Warmth flooded my cheeks. "No . . . But I know she wants to know where he's at."

"Did they have a fight?"

"Uncle Howard lost a wood-working job he had. This is the second one he's lost. That *I* know of. Maybe he's lost more."

"I don't think I need to get involved in a family squabble." He turned his eyes away from me. "Sorry, Jay."

Anger surged through me. Michael was good for nothing. If Daniel were here, he'd help me.

I climbed to my feet and stumbled down the aisle.

Michael came after me and caught my arm. "Jay, wait." He released me and ran his fingers through his hair. "Maybe we can just find out where he's at, and just let your aunt know. Let her take care of it. How's that sound?"

I turned it over in my mind. At least I'd know Uncle Howard was safe. I didn't have much of a choice. At least it was something. I shrugged my shoulders. "Okay."

We walked to his truck, the sun streaming down. The hot air inside of the truck rushed to meet me.

Michael turned to me. "Where should we look?"

"I don't know. I can't imagine."

"How do you expect me to help you?" He looked at me in exasperation, beating the heels of his hands gently against the steering wheel. "Does he have any other family?"

"Yeah, he does. He has a brother who lives in Hartfield, Georgia. That's too far to go, though."

"No, no. It's just about an hour northeast of here. Do you need to tell your aunt?"

"Yes, I need to let her know. Will you take me by so I can tell her?"

"All right." He cranked the truck and pulled from the parking lot.

I studied Michael's profile. "You told me you haven't been going to church."

"No."

"Why?"

"Reasons."

When we pulled into the yard, I gave him a stern look. He simply gazed back, unperturbed. I slammed the truck door with unnecessary force.

I opened the bedroom door quietly. Aunt Liza still slept. She'd probably been up half the night worrying. I decided not to wake her.

Instead, I wrote a quick note, telling her I was with Michael and would be back in a few hours. After I put it under the sugar bowl, I hurried back out.

Chance met me, and I gave him a quick pat on the head before I climbed into the truck.

Chapter 32--Searching

Before we'd even pulled into the road, I cleared my throat. "And?"

"What?" Michael threw a puzzled look at me.

"Your reasons. Why aren't you going to church?"

"Personal reasons." He clenched his teeth together so tightly that a muscle twitched in his jaw.

I sighed and turned to the opened window. The wind blew my hair into tangles. I swept it back with both hands and tied it with a ribbon from my pocket.

Michael's voice startled me. "Why don't you get your hair cut like the other girls?"

"You want me to cut my hair?"

"It's your hair. I don't care what you do with it. I just wondered why you don't cut it like all the other girls I've seen."

"Would it look better cut?"

He frowned at me. "How should I know?"

I smiled. "I happen to like it like this. I don't have to do what all the other girls do."

"No, you don't." His face smoothed as he cast a glance at me.

I made a face at him. "I'm glad you agree."

He didn't answer. A few raindrops splattered on the windshield. I held my head halfway out the window to peer up at the sky.

"Wow. There's a dark cloud building right over us."

He bent his head for a better view through the windshield. "We're going to get some heavy rain from that. Unless we're able to outrun it."

"Maybe it'll cool things off." I pulled my handkerchief from my belt to wipe the rain from my face. "Why were you in the church?"

"I told you to cool off. Just looking for a quiet place."

I sighed. He wasn't going to tell me anything.

We drove twenty more minutes before the rain started coming down in earnest. We rolled up the windows to keep from getting soaked.

The heavy rain drowned out any attempts at conversation--not that Michael showed any interest in talking anyway. The windshield wipers whished back and forth.

The fury of the thunderstorm quickly abated, but heavy drops still fell. I rolled down my window an inch or so, glad for the cool air blowing through. I decided to try again. "How's Sylvia today?"

"She's fine as far as I know."

I raised an eyebrow. "As far as you know?"

He sighed heavily. "Miss Nosey Parker, we broke up today."

"Oh. I'm sorry. I didn't know." So, that's why he was in Plainsville—breaking up with Sylvia. Did that mean his kissing in the backseat yesterday was just a sham? Or, just from being so drunk he didn't know or care what he did?

He rubbed his nose. The rain let up, and the windshield wipers now squealed across the windshield. He switched them off.

He gave me a sideways glance. "Sylvia and I were too different."

I nodded my head.

He raked his fingers through his hair. "I don't understand women. Why would she wear a suit like that?"

"I don't know. Maybe to get attention?" I kept my voice even.

"Maybe. Anyway, she got lots of attention from Andrew." He cut his eyes over to me. "You may not know. Andrew and Marla broke up, too."

"You mean Sylvia and Andrew. . ."

He nodded his head. "Yes." He kept his eyes glued on the road. "Of course, she really wanted attention from Dan. He wouldn't play her game, though."

"She was trying to get Daniel's attention?"

"Yes. You didn't notice? It's been going on for a while."

"What's been going on?"

"She's been after Daniel since she first met him."

"How do you know?"

"Believe me. I know." He cast another glance my way. "She's so jealous of you it's not even funny."

"Of me?" She was the popular one, the pretty one, the one with the cute clothes.

He smiled wryly. "She thought if she dated me she could make Dan jealous. That's why she. . ."His voice trailed off, and he reddened.

"Kissed you?" So, she had been the one. Not Michael. But he hadn't stopped her, had he? I shook my head. "Michael, you're wrong."

He cast me a sideways glance. "What do you mean?"

"Sylvia was after *you*. She told me y'all dated, the weekend you brought the horses, remember?"

He laughed. "Jay, silly girl." He shook his head at me. "She said that to make you jealous. She thought if she made you jealous enough, you'd come back to me. *That you'd dump Dan and concentrate on me.*" The muscle twitched in his jaw again. "She didn't know you actually preferred Dan."

"But I didn't prefer him! You know it wasn't like that. . ."

"No, I *don't* know. I do know this: Daniel never has eyes for anyone but you."

I shook my head. "That's not true. He really likes Marla."

He looked doubtful and shrugged his shoulders. His grip on the steering wheel tightened. "Do you think I. . ."

"What?" I clutched my fingers tightly together.

"Nothing. Forget it." He stared straight ahead.

I shifted my position. "Were you going to ask if I think you can stop drinking?"

He gave me a funny look. "No, that's not what I was going to say." He gritted his teeth. "Don't try to change me, Jay. You used to like me just fine the way I am."

I pressed my lips together and looked away.

Michael sighed. "Dan's really not a bad guy. He used to be my best friend. I know you two will be happy together."

My heart hammered in my chest as I twisted to face him. "Why are you telling me this? Are you blaming me for everything? You broke up with me," I said accusingly.

"I could see what was happening between you and Dan. I knew I didn't stand a chance."

"You were wrong."

"No. I was right. You proved it."

"You pushed me into his arms. You made it happen. Your drinking. . ." My hands shook, and I clasped them together again.

"No. You chose him over me."

"I didn't! You walked away *from me.* For what? You prefer drinking to me."

"What choice did I have? I can't compete with Dan. Never could." He shot me a sorrowful look. "Jay, I can't talk about this anymore."

I pinched the bridge of my nose and closed my eyes.

"Jay. . ." His voice broke.

"You want me to break up with Daniel?" I didn't open my eyes, but I heard him grit his teeth. "And we'll get back together? But you won't stop drinking?" I opened my eyes and turned to face him.

He nodded. "That about sums it up."

I shook my head. "No. Not until you stop drinking. Even then. . ." How could I hurt Daniel, after all he had done for me? After he had been so kind?

"Even if I stopped drinking, you would still choose him?"

"I didn't say that. I don't know."

He shrugged his shoulders. "Then that settles it."

"But, Michael, why do you drink?"

His face clouded. "Why do you think?"

"Don't blame me for your drinking, Michael Hutchinson!"

"I'm sorry. I wasn't blaming you." He rubbed his eyes with the heel of his right hand. "Life is hard. Drinking eases the pain."

"Do you know the pain I've had? And I don't drink." I said the words and was sorry. How did I know what pain Michael had endured?

He glanced at me for a second but did not speak.

I bit my lip. "I'm sorry, Michael. You've never told me about your troubles, and I have no right to assume mine have been worse than yours."

He sighed heavily.

"What?" I asked.

He grimaced but did not look at me. "Your pain *is* my pain." He stared out the windshield at the road.

My heart constricted. Was it easier to endure suffering or watch someone suffer? Did he love me that much, *to hurt when I hurt?* To maybe hurt more? I cleared my throat. "Michael, drinking just causes more pain in the long run-- for everyone."

He shook his head slowly. "Maybe. But I've been drinking so long, I don't know if I can live sober."

"Couldn't you try?"

He shot me a look. "Why? What's the point?"

Clothed In Thunder

He wouldn't even try? My heart broke. I was now sorry I had talked Michael into this trip. I leaned my head out the window again, letting the air flow over me, cooling my hot cheeks.

I wanted Michael to fight for me. *If not for me, for himself.*

Instead, he was just giving up, drowning in self pity.

.

Chapter 33—Michael's Friend

Michael remained silent until we reached the bridge that led to Hartfield. "Do you know where your uncle's brother lives?"

"No."

"Can you remember anything he has said about his brother? Anything?"

I furrowed my brow and held my head between my palms, massaging my temples. "Flatrock. He mentioned Flatrock. That's all I know."

"We'll stop and ask someone."

We spotted a group of people gathered on a street corner, at a bus stop, and Michael pulled over.

I stuck my head out of the window. "Do you know where Flatrock is located?"

The two men shrugged their shoulders. A short woman who was almost as wide as she was tall trotted over to us.

"Flatrock?" she asked.

"Yes, we're looking for Mr. Barnett. He lives in Flatrock."

She shook her head. "Never heard of him. There's no Flatrock in Hartfield that I know of."

My heart sunk. We'd never find Uncle Howard. This was a wasted trip. In more ways than one.

The woman leaned her elbows on the car and peered in at us. "But there is a Flatrock outside of New Hope."

"Really? Can you tell us how to get there?"

"Sure. I can draw you a map if you got paper and pencil handy."

Michael rummaged among his books in the floorboard and came up with a piece of paper and a stub of a pencil.

The woman leaned on the hood of the car and placed the pencil lead between her lips to wet it. She laboriously drew a map.

I gave her a wave as we drove away. I studied the map she had drawn.

Michael tapped his fingers against the steering wheel as we drove along. "Are you going to help me find the streets she marked?"

"Yeah. But I may get us lost. I can't find my way out of a sack."

Sure enough, we had to turn around once when I saw the sign too late, but a few twists and turns later, we found the small community of Flatrock.

The sun peeked out from behind clouds, now hanging low in the sky. It was getting late.

Michael turned down a side road, trying to find someone we could ask. A boy who looked to be in his early teens rode a bicycle in front of us. Michael drove past him, and I jumped out of the truck to flag the boy down.

"Do you know a Mr. Aaron Barnett?"

"Reckon I do. He lives next door to me."

I breathed a sigh of relief. This was easier than I thought. "Do you happen to know his brother, Howard Barnett?"

"I seen him a few times."

"Have you seen him today?"

"Matter of fact, I have. He was at church this morning with his brother."

"Thank you so much. Don't tell him I was asking about him, please?"

The boy's eyes brimmed with curiosity, but he agreed.

"Thanks again." I climbed back in the truck and turned to Michael. "Are you sure we can't go see how he is? Try to convince him to get help for his drinking?"

Michael shook his head. "This is between him and your aunt. None of our business."

"That boy will probably tell him we were looking for him."

"Can't help that. We got to get back, anyway. It's getting late." He backed into a drive to turn the truck around.

"I wish there was someplace we could get something to drink."

He threw a glance at me and shrugged. "Everything's closed on Sunday."

We drove in silence for a few more minutes before Michael spoke again. "I do have a friend from college who lives near here. We can swing by his house if you want to."

"That would be great. I'm about to perish."

"Okay. We'll be there in a few minutes."

Fifteen minutes later, we pulled into the yard of one of the biggest houses I had ever seen. A large porch wrapped around the entire house. Large columns flanked the wooden porch steps.

But the white paint peeled, and the steps sagged. Even though the house and yards were neglected, they still retained a sense of grandeur.

When I walked up the steps with Michael, I felt a chill run up my spine. Fear surged through me, and I fought down the urge to run back to the truck. I stayed close by Michael's side as he knocked on the door.

We heard shuffling of feet, and the door opened revealing a toothless, bent old woman.

"Yes?" Her voice was a whistle through her toothless gums.

"Is Paul home?" Michael asked.

The old woman looked us up and down, scratching a hairy chin. "Wait right here. I'll go get him."

A young man, his hair neatly combed and his face cleanly shaven, appeared at the door a few minutes later. "Michael!" he cried.

They embraced like long-lost brothers.

"Come in, come in." He held the door wide.

Michael glanced at me. "Jay, this is Paul Miller. Paul, Sarah Jane Hunter."

"Nice to meet you," I said. I held out my hand, and his hand grasped mine in a warm handshake.

"Nice to meet you." He grinned at us.

"Sorry to butt in on you like this . . ."

"You're always welcome!"

"Jay was hoping for a drink of water."

Paul smiled. "Come on to the kitchen, and I'll fix you up."

We followed him into a large kitchen, his friendliness doing nothing to ease the feeling of fear still within me. A large table made of knotted pine, darkened with age, stood in the middle of the room. Twelve high-backed, sturdy-looking chairs surrounded it.

Paul pulled out one for me, and Michael sat down across from me. Paul bustled around and brought us glasses of iced tea.

"Are you hungry? I can whip up something." He glanced from Michael to me.

When my stomach growled, Michael and Paul both laughed.

I smiled. "Actually, I haven't eaten all day. If it's not too much trouble. . ."

"No, not at all." He whipped an apron off a peg and tied it around his waist. Then he opened the icebox and got out three eggs. "How about an omelet?"

"A what?" I asked.

"An omelet. I guarantee you'll love it."

"Sure. That'll be great. "

"I'll have it done in a jiffy." He got a match and lit the burner on the stove. "My granny and I are the only two of my family here today. Everyone else has gone to a neighbor's. Their daughter was getting married." He took down an iron skillet that hung from the wall and placed it on the gas stove. "Someone has to stay with Granny. It was my turn today."

Paul seemed at odds with the decrepit house. But, even his charm could not erase the sense of uneasiness I felt as he prepared the omelet.

Chapter 34--The Fortune

The meal was as delicious as Paul had promised. I savored every bite of the omelet. After our meal, we carried our coffee cups to the back porch. The old woman sat there, staring toward a large pond.

"This is my great-grandmother, Esther Miller," Paul said. "Granny, this is Sarah Jane and Michael."

I took her gnarled hand in mine, and she patted my hand with crooked fingers.

It was peaceful on the back porch although getting chilly. An afghan draped over the back of the chair, and I asked if I could use it. Paul nodded, and I wrapped it around my shoulders as I took a seat. The frogs sang at the pond as the dusk gathered. As cool as it was getting, they would soon be gone.

"Good time to fish," Paul said. "Do y'all want to go wet a hook?"

Michael looked at me. "If Jay wants to. . ."

I waved a hand. "You two go. I'll just wait here, if that's okay, Paul."

"Sure. Won't take long to catch a mess of fish. We'll be back in a jiffy."

The two left.

Paul's granny studied me. "When are you and your young man getting hitched?"

"My young man?"

"Michael, weren't it?"

"Yes, ma'am. His name's Michael. But he's not my young man. We're not planning on getting married."

She smiled her toothless grin. "You finished with your coffee?"

I placed it to my lips to drain the last of it. "Yes, ma'am. Did you want me to go get you some?"

"No, no. I'm going to read your grounds."

"Read my grounds?"

"This is what I a want ya to do. Flip the cup upside down and turn it 'round three times, a saying these words. Meech, meech, merach, merash, meech, merash."

My mouth dropped open. Was Paul's granny crazy? She was so old dementia had probably set in. I decided to humor her.

I did as she said, feeling foolish as I said the words. I handed the cup to her. When my fingers touched hers, a thrill ran up my spine, and goosebumps appeared on my arms.

Nevertheless, or, perhaps, because of my unease, I moved my chair closer to hers and leaned to look into the cup as she did. She slowly twirled the cup around in her fingers, not saying anything for a full five minutes. And then she spoke. Surprisingly, her voice no longer whistled. She spoke emphatically and clearly.

"You will marry Michael when his battle with demons ceases. You will have great sorrow when he travels over the ocean. But his faith and courage is strong, and he will come back to you, broken, but not beyond repair. You will be blessed with five children and numerous grandchildren. Thirteen? No, fourteen. Your children will rise up and praise you in your old age. You and Michael will live together for fifty-four years before the Lord calls him home. Again you will grieve, but not as one who has no hope. You will live sixteen more years, still vigorous of mind and body before you meet your Lord and Savior." She handed me back my cup.

I held it loosely in my hands and stared at her. Emotions swirled through me. Hope, anger, joy, and finally disgust. How dare she say these things to me! Feeding me such foolishness. Michael and I would never marry. I knew that now. And why would he travel over the ocean? Ridiculous.

Before I said anything I would regret, I leaped to my feet and hurried back to the kitchen.

I leaned against the counter and peered down at the coffee grounds. They just looked like coffee grounds. Nothing more. I turned to the sink and washed our dirty dishes.

I had calmed some when Michael and his friend came back. But my insides felt like jelly.

Michael and I gave our thanks for the hospitality and walked toward his truck. The temperature had plunged, and I shivered. Michael staggered beside me, and I clutched his arm.

When he came to a stop, I took a sniff, and the unmistakable smell of whiskey assaulted my nose. "Michael!"

He glanced at me, bleary eyed. "What's wrong?"

"You smell like a brewery."

"Paul was drinking. He must have spilled some on me."

"Spilled some down your throat, you mean."

"Why are you so upset?"

"You're in no shape to drive. You're drunk."

"I'm not drunk. I just had a couple of drinks."

"You just lied to me. You said you didn't drink with Paul at all. Now you say a couple. In a minute it'll be four or five drinks." I poked a finger in his chest. "

Michael shook his head. "You're being ridiculous."

Tears began, but I blinked them away. Paul's grandmother telling me I would marry him--a drunk. Why had she told me such foolish things?

My hands shook with anger. "Give me the keys."

"I told you I'm not drunk. I can drive fine."

"I'm not getting in the truck with you unless you let me drive."

"Fine." He yanked the keys from his pocket and threw them to me.

"You're the reason, you know." He didn't bother opening the door for me. Instead, he climbed in the passenger side and slammed the door.

After I got in, I faced him. "The reason for what? Your drinking? I thought we already talked about this."

"No, the reason I'm not attending church." He shook his head slowly, as if clearing away cobwebs. "I don't know if I believe in God anymore. . .I don't understand the world. All the pain and sorrow." He shook his head more vehemently. "I don't understand God."

His words slurred slightly, and he slumped forward in the seat. I felt a pang of compassion, but my anger stuffed it away.

"Why try to understand someone you don't believe in?" I cranked the truck.

He raked his hair back. "I don't know. I just don't understand why he is making me go through this . . . if he does exist."

"Go through what?"

He remained silent for a moment before swinging a hand in dismissal. "Just things. And then that stuff we're learning in biology classes."

"You mean evolution?"

"Yes. Charles Darwin? Wasn't that the guy's name?"

"Yes, but all of that is ridiculous. You can't believe that stuff!"

"I'm not sure what to believe anymore." His eyes surveyed me sadly.

"Michael, I don't know what you're going through. . ."

"No, you have no idea."

"But even in dark times, the light is still there. No matter how deep the night, the sun shines somewhere in the world."

I drove in silence for a few miles before I spoke again.

"Michael?"

"Yes?"

I paused. "Do you think that old woman was peculiar?"

"Paul's grandmother?"

"His great-grandmother," I corrected.

"No more peculiar than anyone else. Why?"

"She told my fortune." I cast a glance in his direction. "I know it was just a bunch of silliness. Still, it was really strange."

"How did she tell your fortune?"

"She read my coffee grounds."

"Coffee grounds? I've heard of tea leaves but not coffee grounds." He laughed.

I shivered. "It wasn't funny. She scared me."

"Did she say something bad was going to happen?"

"No . . . not bad. I guess mostly good things."

"Like what?"

"She said I would have five children . . . things like that."

He laughed again. "It's hard to imagine you with children."

"What do you mean?" I said, indignant.

"Oh, I know you'd be a great mother. You're so good with Zeke. I just mean you're so young."

"Thanks, old man."

He laughed again before he twisted in the seat to stare at my profile.

I tossed a sideways glance at him. "Why are you looking at me like that?"

"I think you need to know something. . ." He stared at me so sorrowfully that it scared me.

"What?"

"Your uncle is not an alcoholic."

"He's not? How do you know?"

"Jay, I know the signs. Your uncle doesn't drink."

Isn't that what Aunt Liza had said? But all the empty bottles in the shop. . .Why were they there? Just because Michael drank didn't mean he knew what he was talking about. There was no other explanation for the bottles.

But there wouldn't be any need to argue with Michael as drunk as he was.

I managed a smile. "That's good to know." I didn't say anything else.

Michael leaned back and soon slept.

I shook my head. Paul's granny was crazy.

Just a crazy old woman . . .

Chapter 35--Returning

Jt was midnight when we pulled up in Aunt Liza's yard. Michael stretched and yawned and looked around in confusion.

The house was ablaze with lights, and three cars were parked out front.

"I wonder what's going on," I said. Chance met me, and I took a minute to pat his sides before walking in with Michael.

The sitting room bulged with people. Aunt Liza broke free from the preacher when she saw me. To my astonishment she burst into tears.

"What's wrong?" I asked.

She swiped at the tears as several people gathered around us, including Daniel.

"Daniel! What are you doing here?"

His face was grim, and he clenched his teeth without speaking.

I turned back to Aunt Liza. "What's going on?"

"I didn't know where you were." She broke into tears again.

"What do you mean? I left a note." I searched the faces circling us.

The preacher pointed a finger at me. "We were organizing a search party to find you. This is not funny, young lady."

"Where have you been?" Aunt Liza asked.

Daniel still hadn't spoken, but he glared at Michael. I looked down at my shoes. Would Aunt Liza want me to say where we had been in front of all these people?

I cleared my throat. "Michael and I went for a ride."

"A ride? You've been gone for hours and hours." Aunt Liza crushed me against her until I could barely breathe.

I loosened her arms from around me. "I left a note on the kitchen table."

The preacher coughed. "Are you accustomed to keeping such late hours?" He, too, glared at Michael.

I strove to keep my temper. "We just lost track of time."

"Since the young lady's safe, we'll say goodnight." The preacher's face still retained the sour look he had greeted me with.

"I'm sorry for all the trouble," I said. "I don't know what could have happened to the note. I'm really sorry."

I got a curt nod from the preacher. Some of the others patted my hands, and two others hugged me as they filed out.

Michael also told us goodnight and walked out with them, only slightly unsteady on his feet. He apologized to Aunt Liza before he went.

Daniel stayed behind. I flopped down on the couch.

"Some of the neighbors brought food. I'll fix you a plate," Aunt Liza said.

"It's okay. I've eaten," I said.

Daniel's face darkened even more at my words.

"Let me get you a glass of tea at least." She bustled to the kitchen.

"Daniel, I did leave a note . . ."

"What are you doing with Michael?" He came closer to the couch. "Marla told me he broke up with Sylvia."

"When did you see Marla?"

He swung an arm through the air. "That doesn't matter. We're talking about Mike."

I patted the couch. "Sit down, and I'll explain."

Instead, he paced up and down the small room. He wouldn't look at me, so I spoke to his profile.

"Daniel, did Aunt Liza tell you about Uncle Howard?"

He shook his head. "What does this have to do with Mike?"

"Michael took me to find Uncle Howard."

Aunt Liza returned with a plate and the glass of tea. "Dan, would you like anything?"

"No, ma'am. I'm not hungry." He adopted a military stance.

I eyed him in exasperation. His face had hardened, and I could tell he didn't believe me.

I ignored him. "Aunt Liza, I need to tell you something." I took the plate and glass from her. "Michael and I found Uncle Howard. He's with his brother and his family at Flatrock."

Aunt Liza sat down, her face expressionless. "Did you talk to him?"

"No, ma'am. I wanted to, but Michael said it would be better not to."

Relief flooded her face and she nodded. "Michael was right. This business between Howard and me doesn't involve y'all." She got to her feet. "If you two will excuse me, I'm going to bed now. It's been a long day."

I placed the plate and glass on the table, stood, and wrapped my arms around her. "I'm sorry, Aunt Liza. I'm sorry I worried you so."

"I know you didn't mean to." She leaned closer to whisper in my ear. "Be nice to Dan. He's been worried sick."

"Yes, ma'am."

I returned to the couch where Daniel had finally taken a seat. He had not even told Aunt Liza goodnight.

"Where's Flatrock?" he asked tonelessly.

"It's outside of New Hope."

He glanced at me for the first time. "It's less than an hour to New Hope from here. You've been gone all day according to your aunt."

"We stopped by the house of Michael's friend."

"Who?" His eyes narrowed.

"Paul Miller. He's a friend Michael knows from college." I sighed heavily. "I'm trying to be patient with you, Daniel. There was no reason for all this commotion." I took a sip of my tea. "I'm tired. We can talk about this later." I picked up my untouched plate. "You'd better be going." I marched into the kitchen and raked my plate into the slop bucket.

Daniel followed me. I drank the rest of the tea and set the glass on the counter.

"I think I'll spend the night in the shop. . .if that's okay."

Someone knocked at the back door. Before I had a chance to respond, Daniel strode over and yanked it open.

"What do you want?" he said, his voice gruff, blocking the door so I couldn't see.

"Who is it?" I asked.

"Michael. Who do you think?"

Michael tried to push by Daniel, but Daniel put out an arm.

"Please, Dan. I need to talk to Jay."

Daniel shook his head. "You need to leave. Now."

I pushed Daniel back. "Let him in! Come in, Michael." I ignored Daniel's angry look. "What's wrong?"

Michael didn't answer. He paced around the kitchen while Daniel and I watched. He paused and raked his fingers through his hair, his eyes glistening in the light.

Fear choked me. I took Daniel's hand in mine without thinking, and his fingers linked with mine.

"Michael. . ." My voice was barely a whisper. I cleared my throat and tried again. "Michael, you're scaring me. What's wrong?"

"It's Chance." His liquid dark eyes found and held mine.

My hands trembled, and Daniel tightened his grip. "Where is he? What's wrong?"

Michael bowed his head. "He's dead."

Chapter 36--Another Loss

J stared at him. "Dead? He was fine just a few minutes ago."

"One of the people leaving must have run over him," Michael said.

I clung to Daniel, my legs like jelly.

Michael raised his head. A muscle quivered in his jaw. "I'm sorry, Jay."

"Where is he?" I asked.

"I left him outside the backdoor."

I went out and pulled the string to turn the porch light on. My hand shook, sending the bulb swinging. Rays of light shivered across the ground.

Chance lay on an old cloth as if he simply slept. I fell to my knees.

I ran my hand over the silky fur, but Chance didn't move. I checked for a pulse, but there was none. I pulled back an eyelid, but no life danced in his unfocused eyes.

Tears streamed down my face. Falling onto the lifeless form, I rocked back and forth on my knees. A hand lifted me.

Daniel's. He wrapped me in his arms, and my tears wet his shoulder.

Michael stood close by, watching us. I pulled away from Daniel and found my handkerchief. I wiped away the tears and turned to face Michael.

"Did you see what happened?"

Michael shook his head. "I was talking to the preacher. Well, to tell the truth, he was giving me a talking to. He was pretty mad." He swallowed. "And everyone else had already left. When the preacher finally said goodnight, I went to my truck. About twenty feet away, I saw him." Michael's eyes glistened in the light from the bare bulb.

I knelt again by the body and felt the broken bones beneath my fingers. He must have died quickly, and, for that, I was grateful.

I stood and clung once again to Daniel.

"Would you like for me to bury him?" Michael asked.

"I can do it," Daniel said.

I sighed heavily. "Both of you can."

"I'll get the shovels." Michael headed to the barn, his gait still unsteady.

"Daniel. . ." I tilted my head up. "I didn't tell you that Michael's been drinking."

"You didn't have to tell me. I know."

"Oh." That was one of the reasons why he was so angry. "I don't think he should be driving. See if you can get him to stay tonight."

"Jay, are you kidding? Let him go!"

"Daniel, could you forgive yourself if something happened to him?"

He didn't speak for a second. He nodded and sighed. "Reckon you're right."

I couldn't bear to see Chance lowered into the ground. "I'm going in. I can't. . ." Through my tears, I stood on tiptoes to kiss his cheek.

Daniel hugged me and kissed my forehead. "You need to get inside anyway. It's getting chilly." He looked over my head, and I knew he was watching Michael. "If he gets out of line, I'm going to deck him," he said into my ear.

"Daniel! Please be nice?" I swiped at my tears.

"I'm sorry." But he didn't sound like it.

Michael stood at the bottom of the steps with two shovels.

"Where do you want us to bury him?" he asked quietly.

"Under the cedar tree. I'm sure Aunt Liza won't mind."

Clothed In Thunder

I knelt again to run my hand over Chance's beautiful face before I wrapped him in the cloth. This time Michael placed his hand under my elbow to help me to my feet.

"I'll see y'all in the morning." I went in without waiting for an answer.

The coffee cup I had used that morning still sat on the counter along with other dirty dishes. Poor Aunt Liza! She had been so worried that she hadn't bothered cleaning the kitchen. How could Uncle Howard do this to her? To add to her troubles, I had worried her so without meaning to.

I idly twirled the cup around in my hands, looking at the dried grounds. Just grounds. How could Paul' granny see anything in them? I saw nothing.

I took my cup to the sink and filled the pan with soapy water and began to wash the dishes.

Poppa, Zeke, now Chance. I couldn't bear any more loss. I bent my head over the pan and wept, my tears splashing into the water.

A knock sounded softly on the backdoor. I tried to speak, to call 'come in,' but words would not come. I heard the sound of the door opening.

"Jay?" Michael whispered.

I kept my head bent over the sink, willing him to leave. His footsteps crossed the floor until I felt him behind me. He wrapped his arms around me and kissed my neck. Shivers ran down my spine.

I turned and moved away from him, breathing quickly. We faced each other, and he closed the distance between us, and pulled me into his arms. His mouth found mine.

I was the first to pull away, although I still clung to his shirt sleeve, breathing heavily.

He tilted my chin and looked into my eyes. "I'm sorry. I shouldn't have done that."

I searched his eyes, seeing only tenderness. I released my grip on his shirt and stepped back. "It's okay." My hands shook as I pushed back my hair.

"Jay. . ."

I shook my head. "I can't . . .Daniel. . ." I took a shaky breath.

We stood for a few minutes in silence. Finally, Michael cleared his throat. "I actually came in to get a quilt. It's turned a lot cooler."

"Oh. I'll be right back."

I walked, my gait almost as unsteady as Michael's had been, to the chifferobe in Zeke's old room. I opened the door and picked up a quilt and gasped.

Under the quilt lay a gin bottle, still half full.

I stared at it for a few seconds and left it, closing the chifferobe door, unsure what to do. Did Uncle Howard have alcohol hidden all over the house?

I returned to the kitchen and handed the quilt to Michael. "Do you need anything else?"

He caught my arm. "You. I need you."

I pulled away and held up a hand. "Don't. .
.I'm with Daniel."

He surveyed me sadly.

I moved another step back. "Goodnight."

He didn't answer but simply slipped out the
door I held open. I closed the wooden door firmly
behind him and locked it. I stumbled to my
bedroom and fell on my bed.

Images of Chances broken body, Michael's
kiss, and Daniel's anger rushed through my
mind.

I touched my lips that still tingled from the
kiss.

Had Daniel seen? Should I tell him? He
would kill Michael. . .No, I couldn't tell him.
Daniel had been so kind to me. But was that
enough? I rolled my head back and forth. What
was I going to do?

I simply didn't know.

Chapter 37--Not Knowing

The next morning, groggy from lack of sleep, I looked around the kitchen. I knew I had placed the note on the table, under the sugar bowl. The bowl was moved out of its regular place in the center of the table. Did Aunt Liza move the bowl without seeing the note? That would be unusual. But she was so worried about Uncle Howard, she could have been distracted.

I looked on the floor, finally getting down on my hands and knees to peer under the stove and the dry sink. There was the note, wedged near the leg of the sink. I picked it up and smoothed it out, placing it under the sugar bowl.

Aunt Liza was still asleep. I didn't awaken her. Instead, I started breakfast, cooking bacon, eggs, and grits. I also made a baker of biscuits.

I went out to Uncle Howard's shop and knocked on the door. Michael opened the door, holding the quilt.

I took the quilt from his hands. "I fixed breakfast for you and Dan."

"Okay."

"Let Daniel know?"

"Sure."

I went in and put the quilt away before I sank into a chair at the table. What was I doing inviting him into the house after last night? But, he had to eat, didn't he?

I went to Aunt Liza's bedroom and knocked on the door. She didn't answer, so I cracked the door and peeked in. She lay on her back, her mouth open, snoring softly. I walked to her bed and shook her shoulder. She opened her eyes a crack.

"Aunt Liza, I cooked breakfast and Michael and Daniel are here."

"Michael and Daniel?"

"Yes, ma'am." I sat down on the edge of her bed and told her about Chance.

She sat up and placed a hand on my arm. "Poor Chance! I'm so sorry, Jay."

Tears stung my eyes, but I blinked them away.

I stood and managed a weak smile. "Oh. And I found the note. It was under the dry sink."

"You didn't have to look for it. I believed you, honey."

"Anyway, I've got breakfast done. You need to hurry before the biscuits get cold."

I went back to the kitchen, and Michael and Daniel were at the screen door, and I motioned them in.

"Aunt Liza will be here in a minute. Would y'all like a cup of coffee?"

"Sure," Daniel said, following me to the stove.

Michael simply nodded and moved to the table without looking at me.

I poured each a cup and placed the creamer and sugar in front of Michael.

"Thanks for the milk and sugar, but I drink it black now." He looked down into his cup, avoiding my eyes, I thought.

I sat down across from him. Daniel took a seat next to me.

Daniel took a sip of coffee, watching me. Finally he spoke. "Feeling better, Jay?"

I simply nodded. Aunt Liza came in and joined us.

She nodded at Michael. "Will you bless our food for us?"

I caught my breath. Why hadn't she asked Daniel? After what Michael had told me yesterday, about no longer believing in God, I was unsure of what he would do.

He hesitated for only a second before bowing his head. "Dear God, Thank you for this food. Bless the hands that prepared it. Amen."

Short, but he had prayed. I passed the biscuits to Aunt Liza, but she waved them away. "I'm not hungry. I'll just have coffee." She didn't say anything else, did not even try to make small talk with Michael or Daniel.

I put my hand on hers. "Do you want to go talk to Uncle Howard?"

She shook her head, her eyes on the coffee cup.

"I could go with you if you want me to. . ."

Her head flew up. "No. It won't do any good."

"You never know unless you try."

She leveled her gaze at me. "Please, Jay. Let's not talk about it."

I pushed the eggs around my plate. "If you really love someone, you can't just give up." I glanced up and saw Michael watching me intently. Warmth flooded my face.

Aunt Liza sighed. "It's not that easy."

I opened my mouth to answer, but Daniel made a slight shake of his head at me, and I fell silent. Now wasn't the time to talk about this. And, Aunt Liza was right. It wasn't easy.

Michael buttered his third biscuit. Maybe he was trying not to hurt my feelings. Daniel was still working on his first one.

I glanced at the clock. "It's getting late. I'm going to be late for the bus."

"I'll take you," Michael said.

I had forgotten for a moment that I attended college with Michael.

Daniel pushed his chair back. "No. I'll take her."

"You're not going down home?" I asked.

"No, I decided to stick around here."

Michael was on his feet moving toward the door. "Thanks for breakfast, Jay. Mrs. Barnett, I'm sorry about yesterday."

She waved a hand in his direction. "I know it was just a misunderstanding."

I started to clear the table, but she stopped me. "Go before you're late. I'll clean up."

"If you're sure. . ." I dropped a kiss on her bent head. "I'll be back as soon as I can." I hated leaving her alone, but I didn't need to fall behind in my classes.

We left Aunt Liza looking into her coffee cup as intently as Paul's granny had done.

Could Aunt Liza see what her own future held? I couldn't. I didn't know what we were going to do.

Daniel drove me to school, and neither of us spoke. He parked the car, and I opened the door.

"I'll walk you to your class," he said.

"That's okay. You don't have to."

"But I want to." He took my books from my hands and grinned. "I'll even carry your books for you."

"Thanks."

When we arrived at my class, I reached for my books. His hand closed on mine, and his fingers wrapped around mine.

"Jay. . ."

"Yes?" I looked at our hands intertwined before looking into his eyes.

"Never mind." He gave me a peck on the cheek, released my hand, and strode away.

A group of girls giggled, and I glanced at them. *Another group just like Sylvia and her friends.* People like that were everywhere.

One girl moved away from the group toward me. "Is that your boyfriend?"

"Yes," I said. "Yes, he is." I raised my chin a little higher as I walked to my desk.

Chapter 38--Knowing

J could barely listen in my classes. I was eager to get back to Aunt Liza. I felt uneasy leaving her alone all day. Finally, my last class, biology, ended.

Michael hovered by the classroom door. "Hey, Jay."

"Hey." I shifted my books from one arm to another.

"Let me take you home."

After that kiss, I didn't want to be alone with him. "Michael, that's not a good idea." I tried to move away, but he stopped me.

"I need to talk to you."

"Why?"

"There's something you need to know."

"Tell me here."

He glanced around. "No. There are too many people around."

"Haven't we said all we need to say?"

"It's not that." His eyes filled with sorrow.

I hesitated, but the look in his eyes finally convinced me. He reached for my books, and I allowed him to take them from my grasp. He reached to take my hand, and the same group of girls passed me, giggling loudly. I ignored them but pulled my hand away and stepped back.

"All right. We'll talk. *Just talk.*"

But, once in the truck, he still didn't speak. Once or twice he glanced my way, yet, he remained silent.

I, too, kept silent. What could I say?

When we pulled into the yard, Daniel's car was parked there.

My eyes widened. I had forgotten he hadn't returned to camp. He would explode if he saw me with Michael again. "Michael, just go." I jumped from the truck and ran up the porch.

Marla met me at the door.

"Marla! What are you doing here?"

"I heard about Chance. I wanted to be sure you're okay." She looked at me solicitously before glancing beyond me. "Hi, Michael."

I gritted my teeth. Why had he followed me?

Michael, unshaven, clothes rumpled, ran his fingers through his hair. "Hey." He looked embarrassed. "Umm...sorry to hear about you and Andrew."

Her eyes swept over Michael, taking in his disheveled appearance, I was sure.

They exchanged a look of commiseration. Marla grimaced. "What a pair! Andrew and Sylvia."

Michael laughed harshly. "Yeah, quite a pair." He raked his fingers through his hair again. "Where's Dan?"

"He's tending to the horses," Marla said.

"Uh. . .okay. I'll go see if I can help him."

He left, and Marla raised an eyebrow. I shook my head.

"Nothing is going on between us. Don't look at me like that."

Her eyes filled with compassion. "Poor, Jay!"

I managed a smile. "Poor, Marla!" I was teasing but was distressed to see tears fill her eyes. "Marla, I'm sorry! I didn't know you cared so much for Andrew."

She blinked the tears away. "I don't. It's not that." She managed to smile. "Anyway, I knew you and your aunt were going through so much, so I brought supper over. Daniel was kind enough to give me a ride."

"Oh, you didn't have to do that! But thank you." I gave her a hug. "Where's Aunt Liza?"

"She's lying down." She placed a hand on my arm. "Jay, I'm worried about her."

"You and me both."

"If there's anything I can do, let me know. I'll see you later."She started toward the door.

"Marla. . .can't you stay? Please?"

She hesitated, worrying her bottom lip. "Will Michael be here?"

"I don't know. Maybe." *If Daniel didn't kill him, that was.*

"I'll stay if you need me." Her eyes searched mine, and I could see the pain in hers. Andrew must really have hurt her.

"I would really appreciate it."

"All right." Her expression once again became serene, but the sadness remained in her eyes.

I hugged her again. "Thank you."

We went to the kitchen to set the table and make tea. I kept glancing out the window, wondering about Daniel and Michael. I let out a sigh of relief when I finally spotted them walking toward the house.

"They're almost here. I'll go get Aunt Liza." I left Marla pouring glasses of tea.

Aunt Liza refused to get up, barely moving when I shook her. She just mumbled she wasn't hungry. So, I left her.

We gathered around the table, and Daniel gave thanks without being asked. Michael and Daniel were calm but seemed preoccupied. Neither spoke much while we ate.

I noticed Daniel downed four of Marla's biscuits, and I felt a pang of jealousy. Well, I could learn to make better biscuits. I just needed a little practice.

After we cleaned up the kitchen, I made a fresh pot of coffee, and we carried our cups to the sitting room. It was cool, but not cool enough for a fire in the fireplace.

I wondered if Michael planned to spend the night again. There would be no need, but he didn't seem to be in any hurry to leave. Thankfully, he didn't appear to be drinking. Then again, maybe he was hiding it.

I shook my head. Michael had told me Uncle Howard didn't drink. Was that true? I thought of the gin bottle in the chifferobe. That didn't seem a likely place for *him* to keep an extra bottle.

But, but. . .*I didn't want to think it.* I shook my head.

"Jay?" Daniel rubbed my arm. "Are you okay?"

I didn't answer. I got up and went to the chifferobe and looked under the quilt. I stared at the bottle.

It was empty.

I took the bottle back with me to the sitting room. I held it out. "I found this. It must. . ." I swallowed. "Aunt Liza . . . She's the one who drinks."

Michael dropped his eyes. Marla's lips tightened.

Daniel stood and took a step toward me. I stepped back, clutching the bottle to my chest. "You knew. All of you knew."

No one spoke.

"Why didn't you tell me?" Tears threatened, but I held them back. "Why?"

Michael spoke first. "It wasn't any of my business." He shrugged.

Marla, her face stricken, spoke so softly I had to strain to hear her words. "I didn't want to hurt you."

Daniel shook his head. "I'm sorry, Jay. I wasn't sure. Michael and I just talked it over today. We were going to tell you tonight."

That's why Michael wanted to drive me home. He was going to tell me.

Well, now I knew.

Chapter 39--Aunt Liza

I straightened and faced Marla. "How did you know?"

She licked her lips. "I guess I've always known. Everyone in town knows."

Everyone knew but me. Images sped through my mind. Marla--watching Aunt Liza and me on the first day of school, Miss Ballard--the concern in her eyes, Principal Martin--helping me with the scholarship, maybe to get me away from my aunt? And Mr. Albertson, staring at us that first day--thinking I was like my aunt.

I shook my head. How could I not know? "I've been living here a year, and I never knew."

Daniel gave me a sad smile. "Jay, I told you people are good at hiding it. Your aunt used vanilla to cover up the smell of alcohol."

"Vanilla?" I moved away from Daniel and sat down heavily on the couch.

Michael nodded in agreement. "People try to cover up the scent."

"But why? Why did she drink?" I looked from Daniel to Michael.

Neither answered.

Marla came to kneel by my side. "There doesn't have to be a reason. My mother told me your aunt drank in high school."

I heard a noise and looked up. Aunt Liza leaned against the frame of the doorway. She came in and took a seat in the rocking chair.

"Marla's right."

No one spoke. Michael and Daniel both started to stand, but she waved them back to their seats. I moved over so Marla could sit by me.

"Y'all may as well hear it." She turned in the rocker to face me. "Marla's mother knew in high school, along with most folks. You know the story I told about your teacher, Mr. Albertson? I was drinking when I stole the speech he had written." She bit her lip. "He knew I drank, but he never told. Still, everyone knew. I wasn't so good at hiding it then."

She moved uneasily under my scrutiny. "It's my fault he treated you so badly, Jay. I guess he thought you might have inherited my genes."

I frowned at her. "But you were salutatorian!"

She shrugged her shoulders. "I started drinking in high school but not enough to hurt anything--at least, I didn't think it hurt. I still kept up with schoolwork. After graduation, Howard and I married, and that's when it really got bad. I wanted babies so badly. . ." A lone tear flowed down her cheek. "I quit drinking. But our own little boy lived less than a year. And, then, I buried three more tiny ones who never drew breath. . ." Her voice broke.

I bit my own lip to keep from crying. "It's okay, Aunt Liza. You don't have to talk about it."

"No. I want to tell you. Your uncle made a beautiful cradle for our first son." She lowered her head into her hands and struggled to control herself. Finally, she raised her eyes. "One morning I went to check on him. Death had taken him. He died in that cradle. I should have checked on him more, heard his cries. It was my fault."

I shook my head. "Sometimes these things happen. It wasn't your fault."

She didn't appear to hear me. "I wouldn't let Howard destroy the cradle, so he hung it up in his shop. My drinking just got out of control with the deaths of those little ones. I had to drink to stop the pain. I would go out to the shop, look at that cradle, and ask God why." She searched our faces as if we might know the answer.

My heart constricted in compassion. "We can't always know why, Aunt Liza. But Uncle Howard stayed with you. Why did he finally decide to leave?" I kept my voice gentle.

"He got an order from a store to make some different things. One was a baby cradle. I couldn't stand the thought. I got drunk and smashed it, along with the other things he had made." She exhaled sharply. "That was the day Daniel brought you home without Zeke." Her eyes filled with tears. "Zeke. . .I missed him so! My drinking just got worse and worse. Howard tried to reason with me. I got so angry I went to his shop and. . ." She shrugged her shoulder. "Just went on a rampage. He can't make a living with me drinking up our last penny. Ruining his work was the last straw." She again lowered her head into her hands and sobbed.

I came to her, wrapped her in my arms, and wept with her.

She lifted her face to me. "Jay, I'm sorry I talked to the neighbors about your momma. I hope you can forgive me."

I looked at Michael, and he stared solemnly back. No, he had not told Sylvia.

Aunt Liza hugged me to her, and we stayed that way a long time.

I helped her back to bed and stayed with her until she slept. When I softly closed her bedroom door, Daniel waited for me.

"Is she okay?" he asked.

"For now. She's asleep." Feet dragging, I headed to the kitchen. "Where's Michael and Marla?" I asked.

"Mike took Marla to tell her parents she's spending the night."

"Oh! I wish she wouldn't. Tomorrow is a school day."

"She thinks you're more important than school." He regarded me thoughtfully. "She's really a good friend."

I nodded my head. "She's one of the nicest people I know."

A knock sounded at the front door.

"That's probably them," Daniel said, going to answer it.

Michael and Marla came in.

Marla slipped into the chair next to me and patted my arm. "Are you okay?"

I simply nodded.

Michael poured a cup of coffee and leaned back against the counter surveying me. "What do you plan to do?"

I shrugged. "What can I do?"

Daniel cleared his throat. "What your aunt did tonight is a start. The first step is to admit you have a problem."

Marla rubbed my arm. "I know it was hard, for you and her, but Daniel's right. The question now is what's next?"

I pushed my hair away from my face with both hands. "I can't expect Uncle Howard to come back. Not after what Aunt Liza told us."

Michael rubbed his unshaven face with his knuckles. "No. That's too much to hope for."

I sighed heavily, looking away. What did Michael expect? I couldn't think of him right now. I pinched the bridge of my nose to ease the headache that throbbed. "I'll have to quit school, find a better job, take care of Aunt Liza some way."

Daniel shook his head vehemently. "No, don't quit."

"I agree with Dan. There has to be a better solution," Michael said.

Marla patted my back. "It's nothing we have to decide tonight. You need to get a good night's sleep. Things may look brighter in the morning."

"I better get going," Michael said.

"You're welcome to spend the night," I offered.

He shook his head. "No, I've overstayed my welcome." And he was gone.

I stared at the door as it shut behind him. *Just one more person to disappear from my life.* He had no reason to ever come back. I would probably never see him again once I dropped out of school.

I remained in the kitchen a while longer, reluctant to leave Marla and Daniel.

Marla took matters into her hands. "Come on. We all need to get some sleep."

We told Daniel goodnight, and he left for the shop.

I helped Marla tidy up the kitchen until she shooed me away. "I'll finish up. Go on to bed."

I paused at the doorway. "You can sleep in Zeke's room. Let me know if you need anything."

"No, *you* let me know if you need anything." She came to embrace me and gave me a gentle push. "Go on and don't worry."

Yet, her own face was pinched and white. I did as she said, totally exhausted. I stumbled to my bed, kicked off my shoes, and pulled the covers over me, too tired to even undress.

Chapter 40--Michael Returns

After breakfast that none of us finished, Daniel, Marla, and I went out to the front porch. I stayed home, not able to face my classes. And, what need was there anyway? I would have to quit, the sooner, the better.

Marla refused to leave me to go to school, although I told her she was being silly. The weather had warmed back up, almost like a spring day.

Aunt Liza joined us, looking wretched. Her eyes were dull and sunken and her face pale. Yet, she had dressed and combed her hair, pulling it back into a bun. At least she was making an effort.

We sat there all morning, mainly in silence. Sometimes Marla and Daniel exchanged a look. Marla had said things would appear brighter in the morning, but it wasn't true. I just didn't see a way out of this mess. Quitting school was the only option.

And no Chance came to lay his head upon my knee, to help me feel better. So much loss! How could I get through this? At least I had Daniel and Marla. And Aunt Liza.

So we sat all morning.

Instead of going inside for lunch, Marla fixed sandwiches and brought them out. Daniel helped and brought out a pitcher of tea and glasses.

I felt an infinite sadness. Along with Poppa, Momma, Zeke, and Chance, I had lost Michael. Or, he had lost me. Either way it was the same. The pain took on a permanence, a heaviness, that I knew would never leave me. Perhaps with time, this type of pain would ease. For now, it felt all consuming.

After our lunch, that, again, none of us finished, we still remained sitting. No one seemed to have the energy to move.

Marla sat with her hands folded in her lap, her ankles crossed, her head slightly bowed. Daniel leaned forward, his elbows on his knees, his hands clasped together.

And, so we remained, as the sun traveled across the sky. When the truck drove into the yard, we all startled, as if awakening from a long sleep.

It was Michael's truck. And he wasn't alone.

Uncle Howard was with him.

Aunt Liza remained seated but kept her eyes on Uncle Howard as they approached the porch. Michael held a box in his arms and Uncle Howard a book.

No one spoke. I held my breath. Aunt Liza gripped my arm.

Michael's face was flushed. He set the box on the ground in front of him and raked his fingers through his hair. He stared at the ground for a moment.

With a visible effort, he raised his head and his eyes sought mine.

"I came to tell you something." He squared his shoulders and glanced toward Daniel. "I am a drunk. I've been drinking since. . .since I was a young'n."

Daniel stood, his face contorted.

Michael held up a hand before Daniel could speak. "No, don't blame yourself. Sure you provided the whiskey, you offered it to me, but it was my choice. I could have said no." He swallowed. "Anyway, that's in the past. What's done is done."

Everyone nodded. Daniel remained rooted to the spot.

Marla stood, glanced over her shoulder at me with that look of determination I knew so well, and linked her arm with Daniel's.

My mouth gaped open. When Daniel placed one hand on her arm, as if claiming possession, I could only blink my eyes in response.

Michael furrowed his brow as he stared toward them and then at me. He licked his lips, swallowed, and gradually his face cleared.

Uncle Howard handed him the book.

Michael turned his attention to Aunt Liza. "Mrs. Barnett, I have something for you. Daniel gave me this book, and I'm giving it to you."

Aunt Liza came into the yard, not looking at Uncle Howard. She took the book from Michael and turned it over in her trembling hands.

Michael cleared his throat."Just a couple of years ago a group of men in Ohio got together to help each other, with God's help, to quit drinking. I don't know why we can't start a similar group here, in Plainsville. The group they formed is called *Alcoholics Anonymous*."

He touched Aunt Liza's arm, and she looked into his face. "The group was formed by men, for men. But I've been thinking. Why can't we start a group here, a group for men *and women*? And, that book can help us get started."

Aunt Liza looked from the book to Michael and then to Uncle Howard. She stepped toward Uncle Howard and searched his face. "Do you mean you'd give me another chance if I help Michael form this group?"

He didn't answer, just opened his arms, and she fell into them, sobbing.

A lump formed in my throat. Marla swiped at tears, and even Daniel swallowed hard. When Aunt Liza took Uncle Howard's handkerchief and wiped her tears away, Michael lifted the box at his feet.

"Jay, this is for you. I hope you will accept it."

In a daze, I climbed to my feet, walked down the steps, and stopped in front of Michael, searching his eyes.

"Go ahead," he urged. "Look."

My gaze fell to the box. An Australian Shepherd puppy lay curled up on an old towel.

"He's yours. If you want him."

I reached into the box and pulled the puppy out. "He looks just like Chance." I looked up into Michael's face. "A second Chance," I whispered.

The puppy yawned, emanating puppy breath. I held him close, and he snuggled beneath my chin. Tears ran unheeded down my face. The puppy squirmed in my arms, his warm tongue licking my chin.

Michael touched my arm. "Jay?"

I raised my eyes to his that burned with such passion that mine closed for a second. When I opened them, Michael had moved closer, his mouth at my ear.

"Will you, Jay? Will you give me a second chance?"

I lifted my face to Michael.

"Yes," I whispered.

His lips brushed mine before he pressed his forehead to mine, holding my face with both hands.

Daniel cleared his throat. "Jay, does this mean you're breaking up with me?"

Marla and Daniel had walked into the yard. Daniel now had his arm draped over Marla's shoulders. Marla beamed at me while Daniel grinned.

"Mutual decision?" I asked, raising one eyebrow.

"Mutual decision," Daniel agreed.

Aunt Liza brushed her tears away. "Everyone stays for supper."

Daniel and Marla started to protest, but she cut them short.

"That wasn't a question," she said firmly. "I want all of you at the table tonight, okay?"

We all nodded agreement. Marla and I offered to help, but she shook her head.

"Howard will help." She smiled at him.

Uncle Howard smiled back and followed her into the house.

"I think they want to be alone," I whispered to Marla.

We giggled and went back to the porch. I sat down next to Michael on the swing, leaning on his shoulder. The puppy sighed once and laid his head on my hand and closed his eyes.

Daniel and Marla drew their chairs close together and held hands.

We swung for a while. Daniel and Michael talked, but I only half-listened, only wanting to experience the joy bubbling within me. Occasionally, Marla and I would smile at one another.

Michael kissed the top of my head. "I'm sorry, Jay, for all I put you through."

"Let's not talk about it. That's in the past, and we don't live there anymore."

He kissed my head again and squeezed my shoulders. "No, and I don't want to go there again. I want to tell you I will do my best, Jay, but it won't be easy. I'm on probation."

I sat up and looked at him. "What do you mean?"

"You may have wondered why I was in your freshman biology class. It's because I failed it when I took it the first time. I missed so many days, hung over. I'm on the verge of flunking out." He ran his fingers through his hair. "And I've spent most of the money I had saved up."

"You will not flunk out. And you will find a job so you can stay in school." I tried to make my expression stern but knew I failed when Michael's lips twisted into a smile.

"I'll try my best," he said.

I leaned back on his shoulder. "No, don't just try. You know you can do it."

He kissed the top of my head again. "I don't deserve you. I don't deserve a second chance."

"None of us do, Michael. But, thank God, we get them."

"Amen," Marla and Daniel said at the same time.

Epilogue

We packed a picnic basket, and Michael strapped it behind his saddle. He had made a small basket to hold our new puppy that we had named Coby. I held the basket in front of me, and we let the horses walk along, not wanting our time together to end.

We had gone over three miles when we came to a strand of trees. Michael's horse led the way down a winding path that ended at a stream.

Michael dismounted and took the basket from me. I slid off. There was a grassy knoll, and we let the horses graze unfettered. The puppy was whining inside the basket. I unlooped the string and lifted him out. He wriggled in my arms, trying to lick my face. I inhaled the sweet smell of puppy.

Michael flapped a blanket and spread it out on the ground. I sat down, cross-legged with the puppy in my lap. He soon clambered out and ran circles around me, occasionally putting his rump up and his forelegs down to play growl at me.

Michael brought the basket and placed it on the blanket.

"Are you ready to eat?" I asked.

"No. Let's just enjoy the peace and quiet a while." He lay down on the blanket and put his head in my lap.

I ran my fingers through his hair, listening to the singing of the birds and the splashing of the stream.

His fingers caught mine, and he looked up at me. "When do you want to get married?"

"You have four more years of college." I longed to be with him, but I knew we had to be sensible.

He shook his head. "If I get permission, I can take extra hours. I'll be finished in a little over three years. I could graduate in December."

"Really? If I did that, I should be finished with my undergraduate classes then, too. I could take my veterinarian courses after we married." I looked at him shyly. "I mean, if you want me to."

He sat up and took my hands in his. "Of course I want you to. I want you to do whatever makes you happy. If you want to be a veterinarian, I'll do all I can to help you."

"I can work, too. More jobs seem to be available lately."

"That will mean we won't be able to see each other as often--working, taking extra classes, plus all the homework."

The puppy clambered in my lap and laid his head across my leg. I pulled one hand loose to rub Coby's head. He closed his eyes and softly sighed.

"He tuckered himself out," I said.

Michael grinned. "We might tucker ourselves out with all that work."

"It'll be worth it in the long run." I tightened my hand around Michael's. "It will, won't it?"

He placed his palm against my cheek and kissed me lightly on the lips. "Just three years. And we'll be together. Until death do us part."

I shivered. The old woman's words. What had she said? He would travel over the ocean? I shook my head. That was foolishness. Still, I had to ask.

"Michael, do you want to go anywhere else?"

"Anywhere else? What do you mean?"

"Move to another state. Maybe visit Europe."

"Nope. I want to stay where my heart is. And my heart is right here with you. *Where it will always be."* His voice was a soft whisper that sent tingles up my spine.

He gazed at me with such intensity, I felt dizzy. I shifted my position to lean against him, to lay my head on his shoulder.

He wrapped his arms around me and hugged me tight.

Finally, I stirred. "We'd better eat our lunch. I need to be getting back."

"I reckon so. Your aunt and uncle will be wondering where we're at." Michael pulled the picnic basket to us, and we divided up its contents.

We ate our lunch and packed up. Before we left, we walked down to the stream, hand in hand. The water danced over the rocks, sparkling in the sun. Then we caught the horses and rode home. I helped Michael take the saddles off the horses before we followed the trail that ended at the cedar tree.

I found Chance's grave and sat down beside it, the puppy in my lap.

Michael came out of the barn and dropped to the ground next to me. He plucked a stray piece of grass and shredded it into pieces. "Jay, do you want to live here after we graduate or move down home?"

"I guess it depends on what happens. If the economy improves, and we can make a go of it, I would like to move back to the farm. I would like to buy it back from Uncle Colt, if we can."

"But you do want to stay in Alabama? Right?" His eyes sought mine.

I nodded my head. "Yes. Alabama's my home. Either here or down home. I just wanted you to know I'll go with you if you wanted to live somewhere else. Wherever you go, I'll go."

"And my people will be your people." He grinned at me. "I was just wondering why you asked if I wanted to live anywhere else."

I hesitated. "I asked because of what Paul's granny told me."

He looked at me in surprise. "Paul's granny? What did she say?"

"I know it's silly. She told me you would travel across the ocean."

"She did?" He laughed. "That's not going to happen. I plan to stay right here in Alabama." He kissed my nose. "And marry you in December. Just wait. December, 1941 will be here before we know it."

And his lips brushed mine gently, and I was reminded of the first time we had kissed. . .

in the shadow of the cedar.

A Word from the Author

For those of us who know our history, we know what happened in December, 1941--the bombing of Pearl Harbor. This *may* put a damper on the wedding plans of Michael and Sarah Jane.

In the Shadow of the Cedar series has been loosely (very loosely) based on my mother's life.

I had always planned three books for the series but am running into a bit of a problem. Book Three, *Thunder in the Shadows*, will begin in September, 1938, and will end in 1942.

I know many (including me) will want to know what happens to them during and after the war.

I've decided to do a spin-off, tentatively titled In the Shadow of the Pines that will follow Grace, Marla's little sister, and Zeke. Look for that series beginning in 2014.

Lord willing.

About the Author

Sheila Odom Hollinghead is a retired science teacher living in south Alabama. Visit her website at Rise, Write, Shine! Sheila has a devotional, Eternal Springs, available at Amazon, Apple, Barnes and Noble, and other book stores. It is a compilation of her blog posts written over a two year period. Or, send her a message at sheilahollinghead@gmail.com.

Thundersnow, In the Shadow of the Cedar, Book One, is available here: Thundersnow on Amazon as well as other websites online.

Thunder in the Shadows, In the Shadow of the Cedar, Book Three, has a tentative publication date of December, 2013. Look for it then!

Made in the USA
Charleston, SC
10 December 2012